1st World Library Literary Society

Giving Back to the World

"If you want to work on the core problem, it's early school literacy."

- James Barksdale, former CEO of Netscape

"No skill is more crucial to the future of a child, or to a democratic and prosperous society, than literacy."

- Los Angeles Times

"Literacy... means far more than learning how to read and write... The aim is to transmit... knowledge and promote social participation."

- UNESCO

"Literacy is not a luxury, it is a right and a responsibility. If our world is to meet the challenges of the twenty-first century we must harness the energy and creativity of all our citizens."

- President Bill Clinton

"Parents should be encouraged to read to their children, and teachers should be equipped with all available techniques for teaching literacy, so the varying needs and capacities of individual kids can be taken into account."

- Hugh Mackay

PART FIRST

O LOVE WILL
VENTURE IN!

CHAPTER I

THE thing that I know least about is my beginning. For it is possible to introduce Ethel Rawdon in so many picturesque ways that the choice is embarrassing, and forces me to the conclusion that the actual circumstances, though commonplace, may be the most suitable. Certainly the events that shape our lives are seldom ushered in with pomp or ceremony; they steal upon us unannounced, and begin their work without giving any premonition of their importance.

Consequently Ethel had no idea when she returned home one night from a rather stupid entertainment that she was about to open a new and important chapter of her life. Hitherto that life had been one of the sweetest and simplest character—the lessons and sports of childhood and girlhood had claimed her nineteen years; and Ethel was just at that wonderful age when, the brook and the river having met, she was feeling the first swell of those irresistible tides which would carry her day by day to the haven of all days.

It was Saturday night in the January of 1900, verging toward twelve o'clock. When she entered her room, she saw that one of the windows was open, and she stood a moment or two at it, looking across the straight miles of white lights, in whose illumined shadows thousands of sleepers were holding their lives in pause.

"It is not New York at all," she whispered, "it is some magical city that I have seen, but have never trod. It will vanish about six o'clock in the morning, and there will be only common streets, full of common people. Of course," and here she closed the window and leisurely removed her opera cloak, "of course, this is only dreaming, but to dream waking, or to dream sleeping, is very pleasant. In dreams we can have men as we like them, and women as we want them, and make all the world happy and beautiful."

She was in no hurry of feeling or movement. She had been in a crowd for some hours, and was glad to be quite alone and talk to herself a little. It was also so restful to gradually relinquish all the restraining gauds of fashionable attire, and as she leisurely performed these duties, she entered into conversation with her own heart—talked over with it the events of the past week, and decided that its fretless days, full of good things, had been, from the beginning to the end, sweet as a cup of new milk. For a woman's heart is very talkative, and requires little to make it eloquent in its own way.

In the midst of this intimate companionship she turned her head, and saw two letters lying upon a table. She rose and lifted them. One was an invitation to a studio reception, and she let it flutter indeterminately from her hand; the other was both familiar and appealing; none of her correspondents but Dora Denning used that peculiar shade of blue paper, and she instantly began to wonder why Dora had written to her.

"I saw her yesterday afternoon," she reflected, "and she told me everything she had to tell—and what does she-mean by such a tantalizing message as this? 'Dearest Ethel: I have the most extraordinary news. Come to me immediately. Dora.' How exactly like Dora!" she commented. "Come to me immediately—whether you are in bed or asleep—whether

Amelia E. Barr

you are sick or well—whether it is midnight or high noon—come to me immediately. Well, Dora, I am going to sleep now, and to-morrow is Sunday, and I never know what view father is going to take of Sunday. He may ask me to go to church with him, and he may not. He may want me to drive in the afternoon, and again he may not; but Sunday is father's home day, and Ruth and I make a point of obliging him in regard to it. That is one of our family principles; and a girl ought to have a few principles of conduct involving self-denial. Aunt Ruth says, 'Life cannot stand erect without self-denial,' and aunt is usually right—but I do wonder what Dora wants! I cannot imagine what extraordinary news has come. I must try and see her to-morrow—it may be difficult—but I must make the effort"—and with this satisfying resolution she easily fell asleep.

When she awoke the church bells were ringing and she knew that her father and aunt would have breakfasted. The feet did not trouble her. It was an accidental sleep-over; she had not planned it, and circumstances would take care of themselves. In any case, she had no fear of rebuke. No one was ever cross with Ethel. It was a matter of pretty general belief that whatever Ethel did was just right. So she dressed herself becomingly in a cloth suit, and, with her plumed hat on her head, went down to see what the day had to offer her.

"The first thing is coffee, and then, all being agreeable, Dora. I shall not look further ahead," she thought.

As she entered the room she called "Good morning!" and her voice was like the voice of the birds when they call "Spring!"; and her face was radiant with smiles, and the touch of her lips and the clasp of her hand warm with love and life; and her father and aunt forgot that she was late, and that her breakfast was yet to order.

She took up the reproach herself. "I am so sorry, Aunt Ruth. I only want a cup of coffee and a roll."

"My dear, you cannot go without a proper breakfast. Never mind the hour. What would you like best?"

"You are so good, Ruth. I should like a nice breakfast—a breast of chicken and mushrooms, and some hot muffins and marmalade would do. How comfortable you look here! Father, you are buried in newspapers. Is anyone going to church?"

Ruth ordered the desired breakfast and Mr. Rawdon took out his watch—"I am afraid you have delayed us too long this morning, Ethel."

"Am I to be the scapegoat? Now, I do not believe anyone wanted to go to church. Ruth had her book, you, the newspapers. It is warm and pleasant here, it is cold and windy outside. I know what confession would be made, if honesty were the fashion."

"Well, my little girl, honesty is the fashion in this house. I believe in going to church. Religion is the Mother of Duty, and we should all make a sad mess of life without duty. Is not that so, Ruth?"

"Truth itself, Edward; but religion is not going to church and listening to sermons. Those who built the old cathedrals of Europe had no idea that sitting in comfortable pews and listening to some man talking was worshiping God. Those great naves were intended for men and women to stand or kneel in before God. And there were no high or low standing or kneeling places; all were on a level before Him. It is our modern Protestantism which has brought in lazy lolling in cushioned pews; and the gallery, which makes a church as

Amelia E. Barr

like a playhouse as possible!"

"What are you aiming at, Ruth?"

"I only meant to say, I would like going to church much better if we went solely to praise God, and entreat His mercy. I do not care to hear sermons."

"My dear Ruth, sermons are a large fact in our social economy. When a million or two are preached every year, they have a strong claim on our attention. To use a trade phrase, sermons are firm, and I believe a moderate tax on them would yield an astonishing income."

"See how you talk of them, Edward; as if they were a commercial commodity. If you respected them—"

"I do. I grant them a steady pneumatic pressure in the region of morals, and even faith. Picture to yourself, Ruth, New York without sermons. The dear old city would be like a ship without ballast, heeling over with every wind, and letting in the waters of immorality and scepticism. Remove this pulpit balance just for one week from New York City, and where should we be?"

"Well then," said Ethel, "the clergy ought to give New York a first-rate article in sermons, either of home or foreign manufacture. New York expects the very best of everything; and when she gets it, she opens her heart and her pocketbook enjoys it, and pays for it."

"That is the truth, Ethel. I was thinking of your grandmother Rawdon. You have your hat on—are you going to see her?"

"I am going to see Dora Denning. I had an urgent note from her last night. She says she has 'extraordinary news' and begs me to 'come to her immediately.' I cannot imagine what her news is. I saw her Friday afternoon."

"She has a new poodle, or a new lover, or a new way of crimping her hair," suggested Ruth Bayard scornfully." She imposes on you, Ethel; why do you submit to her selfishness?"

"I suppose because I have become used to it. Four years ago I began to take her part, when the girls teased and tormented her in the schoolroom, and I have big-sistered her ever since. I suppose we get to love those who make us kind and give us trouble. Dora is not perfect, but I like her better than any friend I have. And she must like me, for she asks my advice about everything in her life."

"Does she take it?"

"Yes—generally. Sometimes I have to make her take it."

"She has a mother. Why does she not go to her?"

"Mrs. Denning knows nothing about certain subjects. I am Dora's social godmother, and she must dress and behave as I tell her to do. Poor Mrs. Denning! I am so sorry for her—another cup of coffee, Ruth—it is not very strong."

"Why should you be sorry for Mrs. Denning, Her husband is enormously rich—she lives in a palace, and has a crowd of men and women servants to wait upon her—carriages, horses, motor cars, what not, at her command."

"Yet really, Ruth, she is a most unhappy woman. In that little Western town from which they came, she was everybody. She ran the churches, and was chairwoman in all the clubs, and President of the Temperance Union, and manager of every religious, social, and political festival; and her days were full to the brim of just the things she liked to do. Her dress there was considered magnificent; people begged her for patterns, and regarded her as the very glass of fashion. Servants thought it a great privilege to be employed on the Denning place, and she ordered her house and managed her half-score of men and maids with pleasant autocracy. NOW! Well, I will tell you how it is, NOW. She sits all day in her splendid rooms, or rides out in her car or carriage, and no one knows her, and of course no one speaks to her. Mr. Denning has his Wall Street friends—"

"And enemies," interrupted Judge Rawdon.

"And enemies! You are right, father. But he enjoys one as much as the other—that is, he would as willingly fight his enemies as feast his friends. He says a big day in Wall Street makes him alive from head to foot. He really looks happy. Bryce Denning has got into two clubs, and his money passes him, for he plays, and is willing to love prudently. But no one cares about Mrs. Denning. She is quite old—forty-five, I dare say; and she is stout, and does not wear the colors and style she ought to wear—none of her things have the right 'look,' and of course I cannot advise a matron. Then, her fine English servants take her house out of her hands. She is afraid of them. The butler suavely tries to inform her; the housekeeper removed the white crotcheted scarfs and things from the gilded chairs, and I am sure Mrs. Denning had a heartache about their loss; but she saw that they had also vanished from Dora's parlor, so she took the hint, and accepted the lesson. Really, her humility and isolation are pitiful. I am going to ask grandmother to go and see her. Grandmother might take her to church, and get Dr. Simpson and Mrs. Simpson to introduce her. Her money and adaptability would do the rest. There, I have had a good breakfast, though I was late. It is not always the early bird that gets chicken and mushrooms. Now I will go and see what Dora wants"—and lifting her furs with a smile, and a "Good morning!" equally charming, she disappeared.

"Did you notice her voice, Ruth?" asked Judge Rawdon. What a tone there is in her 'good morning!'"

"There is a tone in every one's good morning, Edward. I think people's salutations set to music would reveal their inmost character. Ethel's good morning says in D major 'How good is the day!' and her good night drops into the minor third, and says pensively 'How sweet is the night!'"

"Nay, Ruth, I don't understand all that; but I do understand the voice. It goes straight to my heart."

"And to my heart also, Edward. I think too there is a measured music, a central time and tune, in every life. Quick, melodious natures like Ethel's never wander far from their keynote, and are therefore joyously set; while slow, irresolute people deviate far, and only come back after painful dissonances and frequent changes."

"You are generally right, Ruth, even where I cannot follow you. I hope Ethel will be home for dinner. I like my Sunday dinner with both of you, and I may bring my mother back with me."

Then he said "Good morning" with an intentional cheer- fulness, and Ruth was left alone with her book. She gave a moment's thought to the value of good example, and then with a sigh of content let her eyes rest on the words Ethel's presence had for awhile silenced:

"I am filled with a sense of sweetness and wonder that such, little things can make a mortal so exceedingly rich. But I confess that the chiefest of all my delights is still the religious." (Theodore Parker.) She read the words again, then closed her eyes and let the honey of some sacred memory satisfy her soul. And in those few minutes of reverie, Ruth Bayard revealed the keynote of her being. Wanderings from it, caused by the exigencies and duties of life, frequently occurred; but she quickly returned to its central and controlling harmony; and her serenity and poise were therefore as natural as was her niece's joyousness and hope. Nor was her religious character the result of temperament, or of a secluded life. Ruth Bayard was a woman of thought and culture, and wise in the ways of the world, but not worldly. Her personality was very attractive, she had a good form, an agreeable face, speaking gray eyes, and brown hair, soft and naturally wavy. She was a distant cousin of Ethel's mother, but had been brought up with her in the same household, and always regarded her as a sister, and Ethel never remembered that she was only her aunt by adoption. Ten years older than her niece, she had mothered her with a wise and loving patience, and her thoughts never wandered long or far from the girl. Consequently, she soon found herself wondering what reason there could be for Dora Denning's urgency.

In the meantime Ethel had reached her friend's residence a new building of unusual size and very ornate architecture. Liveried footmen and waiting women bowed her with mute attention to Miss Denning's suite, an absolutely private arrangement of five rooms, marvelously furnished for the young lady's comfort and delight. The windows of her parlor overlooked the park, and she was standing at one of them as Ethel entered the room. In a passion of welcoming gladness she turned to her, exclaiming: "I have been watching for you hours and hours, Ethel. I have the most wonderful thing to tell you. I am so happy! So happy! No one was ever as happy as I am."

Then Ethel took both her hands, and, as they stood together, she looked intently at her friend. Some new charm transfigured her face; for her dark, gazelle eyes were not more lambent than her cheeks, though in a different way; while her black hair in its picturesquely arranged disorder seemed instinct with life, and hardly to be restrained. She was constantly pushing it back, caressing or arranging it; and her white, slender fingers, sparkling with jewels, moved among the crimped and wavy locks, as if there was an intelligent sympathy between them.

"How beautiful you are to-day, Dora! Who has worked wonders on you?"

"Basil Stanhope. He loves me! He loves me! He told me so last night—in the sweetest words that were ever uttered. I shall never forget one of them—never, as long as I live! Let us sit down. I want to tell you everything."

"I am astonished, Dora!"

"So was mother, and father, and Bryce. No one suspected our affection. Mother used to grumble about my going 'at all hours' to St. Jude's church; but that was because St. Jude's is so very High Church, and mother is a Methodist Episcopal. It was the morning and evening prayers she objected to. No one had any suspicion of the clergyman. Oh, Ethel, he is so handsome! So good! So clever! I think every woman in the church is in love with him."

"Then if he is a good man, he must be very unhappy."

"Of course he is quite ignorant of their admiration, and therefore quite innocent. I am the only woman he loves, and he never even remembers me when he is in the sacred office. If you could see him come out of the vestry in his white surplice, with his rapt face and prophetic eyes. So mystical! So beautiful! You would not wonder that I worship him."

"But I do not understand—how did you meet him socially?"

"I met him at Mrs. Taylor's first. Then he spoke to me one morning as I came out of church, and the next morning he walked through the park with me. And after that—all was easy enough."

"I see. What does your father and mother think—or rather, what do they say?"

"Father always says what he thinks, and mother thinks and says what I do. This condition simplified matters very much. Basil wrote to father, and yesterday after dinner he had an interview with him. I expected it, and was quite prepared for any climax that might come. I wore my loveliest white frock, and had lilies of the valley in my hair and on my breast; and father called me 'his little angel' and piously wondered 'how I could be his daughter.' All dinner time I tried to be angelic, and after dinner I sang 'Little Boy Blue' and some of the songs he loves; and I felt, when Basil's card came in, that I had prepared the proper atmosphere for the interview."

"You are really very clever, Dora."

"I tried to continue singing and playing, but I could not; the notes all ran together, the words were lost. I went to mother's side and put my hand in hers, and she said softly: 'I can hear your father storming a little, but he will settle down the quicker for it. I dare say he will bring Mr. Stanhope in here before long."

"Did he?"

"No. That was Bryce's fault. How Bryce happened to be in the house at that hour, I cannot imagine; but it seems to be natural for him to drop into any interview where he can make trouble. However, it turned out all for the best, for when mother heard Bryce's voice above all the other sounds, she said, 'Come Dora, we shall have to interfere now.' Then I was delighted. I was angelically dressed, and I felt equal to the interview."

"Do you really mean that you joined the three quarreling men?"

"Of course. Mother was quite calm—calm enough to freeze a tempest—but she gave father a look he comprehended. Then she shook hands with Basil, and would have made some remark to Bryce, but with his usual impertinence he took the initiative, and told he: very authoritatively to 'retire and take me with her'—calling me that 'demure little flirt' in a tone that was very offensive. You should have seen father blaze into anger at his words. He told Bryce to remember that 'Mr. Ben Denning owned the house, and that Bryce had four or five rooms in it by his courtesy.' He said also that the 'ladies present were Mr. Ben Denning's wife and daughter, and that it was impertinent in him to order them out of his parlor, where they were always welcome.' Bryce was white with passion, but he answered in his affected way—'Sir, that sly girl with her pretended piety and her sneak of a lover is my sister, and I shall not permit her to disgrace my family without making a protest.'"

"And then?"

"I began to cry, and I put my arms around father's neck and said he must defend me; that I was not 'sly,' and Basil was not 'a sneak,' and father kissed me, and said he would settle with any man, and every man, who presumed to call me either sly or a flirt."

"I think Mr. Denning acted beautifully. What did Bryce say?"

"He turned to Basil, and said: 'Mr. Stanhope, if you are not a cad, you will leave the house. You have no right to intrude yourself into family affairs and family quarrels.' Basil had seated mother, and was standing with one hand on the back of her chair, and he did not answer Bryce—there was no need, father answered quick enough. He said Mr. Stanhope had asked to become one of the family, and for his part he would welcome him freely; and then he asked mother if she was of his mind, and mother smiled and reached her hand backward to Basil. Then father kissed me again, and somehow Basil's arm was round me, and I know I looked lovely—almost like a bride! Oh, Ethel, it was just heavenly!"

"I am sure it was. Did Bryce leave the room then?"

"Yes; he went out in a passion, declaring he would never notice me again. This morning at breakfast I said I was sorry Bryce felt so hurt, but father was sure Bryce would find plenty of consolation in the fact that his disapproval of my choice would excuse him from giving me a wedding present. You know Bryce is a mean little miser!"

"On the contrary, I thought he was very; luxurious and extravagant."

"Where Bryce is concerned, yes; toward everyone else his conduct is too mean to consider. Why, father makes him an allowance of $20,000 a year and he empties father's cigar boxes whenever he can do so without—"

"Let us talk about Mr. Stanhope he is far more interesting.

When are you going to marry him?"

"In the Spring. Father is going to give me some money and I have the fortune Grandmother Cahill left me. It has been well invested, and father told me this morning I was a fairly rich little woman. Basil has some private fortune, also his stipend—we shall do very well. Basil's family is one of the finest among the old Boston aristocrats, and he is closely connected with the English Stanhopes, who rank with the greatest of the nobility."

"I wish Americans would learn to rely on their own nobility. I am tired of their everlasting attempts to graft on some English noble family. No matter how great or clever a man may be, you are sure to read of his descent from some Scottish chief or English earl."

"They can't help their descent, Ethel."

"They need not pin all they have done on to it. Often father frets me in the same way. If he wins a difficult case, he does it naturally, because he is a Rawdon. He is handsome, gentlemanly, honorable, even a perfect horseman, all because, being a Rawdon, he was by nature and inheritance compelled to such perfection. It is very provoking, Dora, and if I were you I would not allow Basil to begin a song about 'the English Stanhopes.' Aunt Ruth and I get very tired often of the English Rawdons, and are really thankful for the separating Atlantic."

"I don't think I shall feel in that way, Ethel. I like the nobility; so does father, he says the Dennings are a fine old family."

"Why talk of genealogies when there is such a man as Basil Stanhope to consider? Let us grant him perfection and agree

Amelia E. Barr

that he is to marry you in the Spring; well then, there is the ceremony, and the wedding garments! Of course it is to be a church wedding?"

"We shall be married in Basil's own church. I can hardly eat or sleep for thinking of the joy and the triumph of it! There will be women there ready to eat their hearts with envy—I believe indeed, Ethel, that every woman in the church is in love with Basil."

"You have said that before, and I am sure you are wrong. A great many of them are married and are in love with their own husbands; and the kind of girls who go to St. Jude's are not the kind who marry clergymen. Mr. Stanhope's whole income would hardly buy their gloves and parasols."

"I don't think you are pleased that I am going to marry. You must not be jealous of Basil. I shall love you just the same."

"Under no conditions, Dora, would I allow jealousy to trouble my life. All the same, you will not love me after your marriage as you have loved me in the past. I shall not expect it."

Passionate denials of this assertion, reminiscences of the past, assurances for the future followed, and Ethel accepted them without dispute and without faith. But she understood that the mere circumstance of her engagement was all that Dora could manage at present; and that the details of the marriage merged themselves constantly in the wonderful fact that Basil Stanhope loved her, and that some time, not far off, she was going to be his wife. This joyful certainty filled her heart and her comprehension, and she had a natural reluctance to subject it to the details of the social and religious ceremonies necessary, Such things permitted others to participate in her joy, and she resented the idea. For a time she wished to keep her lover in a world where no other thought might trouble the thought of Dora.

Ethel understood her friend's mood, and was rather relieved when her carriage arrived. She felt that her presence was preventing Dora's absolute surrender of herself to thoughts of her lover, and all the way home she marveled at the girl's infatuation, and wondered if it would be possible for her to fall into such a dotage of love for any man. She answered this query positively—"No, if I should lose my heart, I shall not therefore lose my head"—and then, before she could finish assuring herself of her determinate wisdom, some mocking lines she had often quoted to love-sick girls went laughing through her memory—

"O Woman! Woman! O our frail, frail sex!
No wonder tragedies are made from us!
Always the same—nothing but loves and cradles."

She found Ruth Bayard dressed for dinner, but her father was not present. That was satisfactory, for he was always a little impatient when the talk was of lovers and weddings; and just then this topic was uppermost in Ethel's mind.

"Ruth," she said, "Dora is engaged," and then in a few sentences she told the little romance Dora had lived for the past year, and its happy culmination. "Setting money aside, I think he will make a very suitable husband. What do you think, Ruth?"

"From what I know of Mr. Stanhope, I should doubt it. I am sure he will put his duties before every earthly thing, and I am sure Dora will object to that. Then I wonder if Dora is made on a pattern large enough to be the moneyed partner in matrimony. I should think Mr. Stanhope was a proud man."

"Dora says he is connected with the English noble family

of Stanhopes."

"We shall certainly have all the connections of the English nobility in America very soon now—but why does he marry Dora? Is it her money?"

"I think not. I have heard from various sources some fine things of Basil Stanhope. There are many richer girls than Dora in St. Jude's. I dare say some one of them would have married him."

"You are mistaken. Do you think Margery Starey, Jane Lewes, or any of the girls of their order would marry a man with a few thousands a year? And to marry for love is beyond the frontiers of such women's intelligence. In their creed a husband is a banker, not a man to be loved and cared for. You know how much of a banker Mr. Stanhope could be."

"Bryce Denning is very angry at what he evidently considers his sister's mesalliance."

"If Mr. Stanhope is connected with the English Stanhopes, the mesalliance must be laid to his charge."

"Indeed the Dennings have some pretenses to good lineage, and Bryce spoke of his sister 'disgracing his family by her contemplated marriage.'"

"His family! My dear Ethel, his grandfather was a manufacturer of tin tacks. And now that we have got as far away as the Denning's grandfather, suppose we drop the subject."

"Content; I am a little tired of the clan Denning—that is their original name Dora says. I will go now and dress for dinner."

Then Ruth rose and looked inquisitively around the room. It

was as she wished it to be—the very expression of elegant comfort—warm and light, and holding the scent of roses: a place of deep, large chairs with no odds and ends to worry about, a room to lounge and chat in, and where the last touch of perfect home freedom was given by a big mastiff who, having heard the door-bell ring, strolled in to see who had called.

Amelia E. Barr

CHAPTER II

DURING dinner both Ruth and Ethel were aware of some sub-interest in the Judge's manner; his absent-mindedness was unusual, and once Ruth saw a faint smile that nothing evident could have induced. Unconsciously also he set a tone of constraint and hurry; the meal was not loitered over, the conversation flagged, and all rose from the table with a sense of relief; perhaps, indeed, with a feeling of expectation.

They entered the parlor together, and the mastiff rose to meet them, asking permission to remain with the little coaxing push of his nose which brought the ready answer:

"Certainly, Sultan. Make yourself comfortable."

Then they grouped themselves round the fire, and the Judge lit his cigar and looked at Ethel in a way that instantly brought curiosity to the question:

"You have a secret, father," she said. "Is it about grandmother?"

"It is news rather than a secret, Ethel. And grandmother has a good deal to do with it, for it is about her family—the Mostyns."

"Oh!"

The tone of Ethel's "Oh!" was not encouraging, and Ruth's look of interest held in abeyance was just as chilling. But something like this attitude had been expected, and Judge Rawdon was not discouraged by it; he knew that youth is capable of great and sudden changes, and that its ability to find reasonable motives for them is unlimited, so he calmly continued:

"You are aware that your grandmother's name before marriage was Rachel Mostyn?"

"I have seen it a thousand times at the bottom of her sampler, father, the one that is framed and hanging in her morning room—Rachel Mostyn, November, Anno Domini, 1827."

"Very well. She married George Rawdon, and they came to New York in 1834. They had a pretty house on the Bowling Green and lived very happily there. I was born in 1850, the youngest of their children. You know that I sign my name Edward M. Rawdon; it is really Edward Mostyn Rawdon."

He paused, and Ruth said, "I suppose Mrs. Rawdon has had some news from her old home?"

"She had a letter last night, and I shall probably receive one to-morrow. Frederick Mostyn, her grand-nephew, is coming to New York, and Squire Rawdon, of Rawdon Manor, writes to recommend the young man to our hospitality."

"But you surely do not intend to invite him here, Edward. I think that would not do."

"He is going to the Holland House. But he is our kinsman, and therefore we must be hospitable."

"I have been trying to count the kinship. It is out of my reckoning," said Ethel. "I hope at least he is nice and presentable."

"The Mostyns are a handsome family. Look at your grandmother. And Squire Rawdon speaks very well of Mr. Mostyn. He has taken the right side in politics, and is likely to make his mark. They were always great sportsmen, and I dare say this representative of the family is a good-looking fellow, well-mannered, and perfectly dressed."

Ethel laughed. "If his clothes fit him he will be an English wonder. I have seen lots of Englishmen; they are all frights as to trousers and vests. There was Lord Wycomb, his broadcloths and satins and linen were marvels in quality, but the make! The girls hated to be seen walking with him, and he would walk—'good for the constitution,' was his explanation for all his peculiarities. The Caylers were weary to death of them."

"And yet," said Ruth, "they sang songs of triumph when Lou Cayler married him."

"That was a different thing. Lou would make him get 'fits' and stop wearing sloppy, baggy arrangements. And I do not suppose the English lord has now a single peculiarity left, unless it be his constitutional walk—that, of course. I have heard English babies get out of their cradles to take a constitutional."

During this tirade Ruth had been thinking. "Edward," she asked, "why does Squire Rawdon introduce Mr. Mostyn? Their relationship cannot be worth counting."

"There you are wrong, Ruth." He spoke with a little excitement. "Englishmen never deny matrimonial relationships, if they are worthy ones. Mostyn and Rawdon are bound together by many a gold wedding ring; we reckon such ties relationships. Squire Raw-don lost his son and his two grandsons a year ago. Perhaps this young man may eventually stand in their place. The Squire is nearly eighty years old; he is the last of the English Rawdons—at least of our branch of it."

"You suppose this Mr. Mostyn may become Squire of Rawdon Manor?"

"He may, Ruth, but it is not certain. There is a large mortgage on the Manor."

"Oh!"

Both girls made the ejaculation at the same moment, and in both voices there was the same curious tone of speculation. It was a cry after truth apprehended, but not realized. Mr. Rawdon remained silent; he was debating with himself the advisability of further confidence, but he came quickly to the conclusion that enough had been told for the present. Turning to Ethel, he said: "I suppose girls have a code of honor about their secrets. Is Dora Denning's 'extraordinary news' shut up in it?"

"Oh, no, father. She is going to be married. That is all."

"That is enough. Who is the man?"

"Reverend Mr. Stanhope."

"Nonsense!"

"Positively."

"I never heard anything more ridiculous. That saintly young

priest! Why, Dora will be tired to death of him in a month. And he? Poor fellow!"

"Why poor fellow? He is very much in love with her."

"It is hard to understand. St. Jerome's love 'pale with midnight prayer' would be more believable than the butterfly Dora. Goodness, gracious! The idea of that man being in love! It pulls him down a bit. I thought he never looked at a woman."

"Do you know him, father?"

"As many people know him—by good report. I know that he is a clergyman who believes what he preaches. I know a Wall Street broker who left St. Jude's church because Mr. Stanhope's sermons on Sunday put such a fine edge on his conscience that Mondays were dangerous days for him to do business on. And whatever Wall Street financiers think of the Bible personally, they do like a man who sticks to his colors, and who holds intact the truth committed to him. Stanhope does this emphatically; and he is so well trusted that if he wanted to build a new church he could get all the money necessary, from Wall Street men in an hour. And he is going to marry! Going to marry Dora Denning! It is 'extraordinary news,' indeed!"

Ethel was a little offended at such unusual surprise. "I think you don't quite understand Dora," she said. "It will be Mr. Stanhope's fault if she is not led in the right way; for if he only loves and pets her enough he may do all he wishes with her. I know, I have both coaxed and ordered her for four years—sometimes one way is best, and sometimes the other."

"How is a man to tell which way to take? What do her

parents think of the marriage?"

"They are pleased with it."

"Pleased with it! Then I have nothing more to say, except that I hope they will not appeal to me on any question of divorce that may arise from such an unlikely marriage."

"They are only lovers yet, Edward," said Ruth. "It is not fair, or kind, to even think of divorce."

"My dear Ruth, the fashionable girl of today accepts marriage with the provision of divorce."

"Dora is hardly one of that set."

"I hope she may keep out of it, but marriage will give her many opportunities. Well, I am sorry for the young priest. He isn't fit to manage a woman like Dora Denning. I am afraid he will get the worst of it."

"I think you are very unkind, father. Dora is my friend, and I know her. She is a girl of intense feelings and very affectionate. And she has dissolved all her life and mind in Mr. Stanhope's life and mind, just as a lump of sugar is dissolved in water."

Ruth laughed. "Can you not find a more poetic simile, Ethel?"

"It will do. This is an age of matter; a material symbol is the proper thing."

"I am glad to hear she has dissolved her mind in Stanhope's," said Judge Rawdon. "Dora's intellect in itself is childish. What did the man see in her that he should desire her?"

Amelia E. Barr

"Father, you never can tell how much brains men like with their beauty. Very little will do generally. And Dora has beauty—great beauty; no one can deny that. I think Dora is giving up a great deal. To her, at least, marriage is a state of passing from perfect freedom into the comparative condition of a slave, giving up her own way constantly for some one else's way."

"Well, Ethel, the remedy is in the lady's hands. She is not forced to marry, and the slavery that is voluntary is no hardship. Now, my dear, I have a case to look over, and you must excuse me to-night. To-morrow we shall know more concerning Mr. Mostyn, and it is easier to talk about certainties than probabilities."

But if conversation ceased about Mr. Mostyn, thought did not; for, a couple of hours afterwards, Ethel tapped at her aunt's door and said, "Just a moment, Ruth."

"Yes, dear, what is it?"

"Did you notice what father said about the mortgage on Rawdon Manor'"

"Yes."

"He seemed to know all about it."

"I think he does know all about it."

"Do you think he holds it?"

"He may do so—it is not unlikely."

"Oh! Then Mr. Fred Mostyn, if he is to inherit Rawdon, would like the mortgage removed?"

"Of course he would."

"And the way to remove it would be to marry the daughter of the holder of the mortgage?"

"It would be one way."

"So he is coming to look me over. I am a matrimonial possibility. How do you like that idea, Aunt Ruth?"

"I do not entertain it for a moment. Mr. Mostyn may not even know of the mortgage. When men mortgage their estates they do not make confidences about the matter, or talk it over with their friends. They always conceal and hide the transaction. If your father holds the mortgage, I feel sure that no one but himself and Squire Rawdon know anything about it. Don't look at the wrong side of events, Ethel; be content with the right side of life's tapestry. Why are you not asleep? What are you worrying about?"

"Nothing, only I have not heard all I wanted to hear."

"And perhaps that is good for you."

"I shall go and see grandmother first thing in the morning."

"I would not if I were you. You cannot make any excuse she will not see through. Your father will call on Mr. Mostyn to-morrow, and we shall get unprejudiced information."

"Oh, I don't know that, Ruth. Father is intensely American three hundred and sixty-four days and twenty-three hours in a year, and then in the odd hour he will flare up Yorkshire like a conflagration."

"English, you mean?"

"No. Yorkshire IS England to grandmother and father. They don't think anything much of the other counties, and people from them are just respectable foreigners. You may depend upon it, whatever grandmother says of Mr. Fred Mostyn, father will believe it, too."

"Your father always believes whatever your grandmother says. Good night, dear."

"Good night. I think I shall go to grandmother in the morning. I know how to manage her. I shall meet her squarely with the truth, and acknowledge that I am dying with curiosity about Mr. Mostyn."

"And she will tease and lecture you, say you are 'not sweetheart high yet, only a little maid,' and so on. Far better go and talk with Dora. To-morrow she will need you, I am sure. Ethel, I am very sleepy. Good night again, dear."

"Good night!" Then with a sudden animation, "I know what to do, I shall tell grandmother about Dora's marriage. It is all plain enough now. Good night, Ruth." And this good night, though dropping sweetly into the minor third, had yet on its final inflection something of the pleasant hopefulness of its major key—it expressed anticipation and satisfaction.

What happened in the night session she could not tell, but she awoke with a positive disinclination to ask a question about Mr. Mostyn. "I have received orders from some one," she said to Ruth; "I simply do not care whether I ever see or hear of the man again. I am going to Dora, and I may not come home until late. You know they will depend upon me for every suggestion."

In fact, Ethel did not return home until the following day, for a snowstorm came up in the afternoon, and the girl was weary with planning and writing, and well inclined to eat with Dora the delicate little dinner served to them in Dora's private parlor. Then about nine o'clock Mr. Stanhope called, and Ethel found it pleasant enough to watch the lovers and listen to Mrs. Denning's opinions of what had been already planned. And the next day she seemed to be so absolutely necessary to the movement of the marriage preparations, that it was nearly dark before she was permitted to return home.

It was but a short walk between the two houses, and Ethel was resolved to have the refreshment of the exercise. And how good it was to feel the pinch of the frost and the gust of the north wind, and after it to come to the happy portal of home, and the familiar atmosphere of the cheerful hall, and then to peep into the firelit room in which Ruth lay dreaming in the dusky shadows.

"Ruth, darling!"

"Ethel! I have just sent for you to come home." Then she rose and took Ethel in her arms. "How delightfully cold you are! And what rosy cheeks! Do you know that we have a little dinner party?"

"Mr. Mostyn?"

"Yes, and your grandmother, and perhaps Dr. Fisher—the Doctor is not certain."

"And I see that you are already dressed. How handsome you look! That black lace dress, with the dull gold ornaments, is all right."

"I felt as if jewels would be overdress for a family dinner."

"Yes, but jewels always snub men so completely. It is not

altogether that they represent money; they give an air of royalty, and a woman without jewels is like an uncrowned queen—she does not get the homage. I can't account for it, but there it is. I shall wear my sapphire necklace. What did father say about our new kinsman?"

"Very little. It was impossible to judge from his words what he thought. I fancied that he might have been a little disappointed."

"I should not wonder. We shall see."

"You will be dressed in an hour?"

"In less time. Shall I wear white or blue?"

"Pale blue and white flowers. There are some white violets in the library. I have a red rose. We shall contrast each other very well."

"What is it all about? Do we really care how we look in the eyes of this Mr. Mostyn?"

"Of course we care. We should not be women if we did not care. We must make some sort of an impression, and naturally we prefer that it should be a pleasant one."

"If we consider the mortgage—"

"Nonsense! The mortgage is not in it."

"Good-by. Tell Mattie to bring me a cup of tea upstairs. I will be dressed in an hour."

The tea was brought and drank, and Ethel fell asleep while her maid prepared every item for her toilet. Then she spoke to her mistress, and Ethel awakened, as she always did, with a smile; nature's surest sign of a radically sweet temper. And everything went in accord with the smile; her hair fell naturally into its most becoming waves, her dress into its most graceful folds; the sapphire necklace matched the blue of her happy eyes, the roses of youth were on her cheeks, and white violets on her breast. She felt her own beauty and was glad of it, and with a laughing word of pleasure went down to the parlor.

Madam Rawdon was standing before the fire, but when she heard the door open she turned her face toward it.

"Come here, Ethel Rawdon," she said, "and let me have a look at you." And Ethel went to her side, laid her hand lightly on the old lady's shoulder and kissed her cheek. "You do look middling well," she continued, "and your dress is about as it should be. I like a girl to dress like a girl—still, the sapphires. Are they necessary?"

"You would not say corals, would you, grandmother? I have those you gave me when I was three years old."

"Keep your wit, my dear, for this evening. I should not wonder but you might need it. Fred Mostyn is rather better than I expected. It was a great pleasure to see him. It was like a bit of my own youth back again. When you are a very old woman there are few things sweeter, Ethel."

"But you are not an old woman, grandmother."

Nor was she. In spite of her seventy-five years she stood erect at the side of her grand-daughter. Her abundant hair was partly gray, but the gray mingled with the little oval of costly lace that lay upon it, and the effect was soft and fair as powdering. She had been very handsome, and her beauty lingered as the beauty of some flowers linger, in fainter tints and in less firm outlines; for she had never fallen from that "grace of God vouchsafed to children," and therefore she had kept not only the enthusiasms of her youth, but that sweet promise of the "times of restitution" when the child shall die one hundred years old, because the child-heart shall be kept in all its freshness and trust. Yes, in Rachel Rawdon's heart the well-springs of love and life lay too deep for the frosts of age to touch. She would be eternally young before she grew old.

She sat down as Ethel spoke, and drew the girl to her side. "I hear your friend is going to marry," she said.

"Dora? Yes."

"Are you sorry?"

"Perhaps not. Dora has been a care to me for four years. I hope her husband may manage her as well as I have done."

"Are you afraid he will not?"

"I cannot tell, grandmother. I see all Dora's faults. Mr. Stanhope is certain that she has no faults. Hitherto she has had her own way in everything. Excepting myself, no one has ventured to contradict her. But, then, Dora is over head and ears in love, and love, it is said, makes all things easy to bear and to do."

"One thing, girls, amazes me—it is how readily women go to church and promise to love, honor, and obey their husbands, when they never intend to do anything of the kind."

"There is a still more amazing thing, Madam," answered Ruth; "that is that men should be so foolish as to think, or hope, they perhaps might do so."

"Old-fashioned women used to manage it some way or other, Ruth. But the old-fashioned woman was a very soft-hearted creature, and, maybe, it was just as well that she was."

"But Woman's Dark Ages are nearly over, Madam; and is not the New Woman a great improvement on the Old Woman?"

"I haven't made up my mind yet, Ruth, about the New Woman. I notice one thing that a few of the new kind have got into their pretty heads, and that is, that they ought to have been men; and they have followed up that idea so far that there is now very little difference in their looks, and still less in their walk; they go stamping along with the step of an athlete and the stride of a peasant on fresh plowed fields. It is the most hideous of walks imaginable. The Grecian bend, which you cannot remember, but may have heard of, was a lackadaisical, vulgar walking fad, but it was grace itself compared with the hideous stride which the New Woman has acquired on the golf links or somewhere else."

"But men stamp and stride in the same way, grandmother."

"A long stride suits a man's anatomy well enough; it does not suit a woman's—she feels every stride she takes, I'll warrant her."

"If she plays golf—"

"My dear Ethel, there is no need for her to play golf. It is a man's game and was played for centuries by men only. In Scotland, the home of golf, it was not thought nice for women to even go to the links, because of the awful language they were likely to hear."

"Then, grandmother, is it not well for ladies to play golf if it keeps men from using 'awful language' to each other)"

"God love you, child! Men will think what they dare not speak."

"If we could only have some new men!" sighed Ethel. "The lover of to-day is just what a girl can pick up; he has no wit and no wisdom and no illusions. He talks of his muscles and smells of cigarettes—perhaps of whisky"—and at these words, Judge Rawdon, accompanied by Mr. Fred Mostyn, entered the room.

The introductions slipped over easily, they hardly seemed to be necessary, and the young man took the chair offered as naturally as if he had sat by the hearth all his life. There was no pause and no embarrassment and no useless polite platitudes; and Ethel's first feeling about her kinsman was one of admiration for the perfect ease and almost instinctive at-homeness with which he took his place. He had come to his own and his own had received him; that was the situation, a very pleasant one, which he accepted with the smiling trust that was at once the most perfect and polite of acknowledgments.

"So you do not enjoy traveling?" said Judge Rawdon as if continuing a conversation.

"I think it the most painful way of taking pleasure, sir—that is the actual transit. And sleeping cars and electric-lighted steamers and hotels do not mitigate the suffering. If Dante was writing now he might depict a constant round of personally conducted tours in Purgatory. I should think the punishment adequate for any offense. But I like arriving at places. New York has given me a lot of new sensations to-day, and I have forgotten the transit troubles already."

He talked well and temperately, and yet Ethel could not avoid the conclusion that he was a man of positive character and uncompromising prejudices. And she also felt a little disappointed in his personality, which contradicted her ideal of a Yorkshire squire. For he was small and slender in stature, and his face was keen and thin, from the high cheek bones to the sharp point of the clean-shaven chin. Yet it was an interesting face, for the brows were broad and the eyes bright and glancing. That his nature held the opposite of his qualities was evident from the mouth, which was composed and discreet and generally clothed with a frank smile, negatived by the deep, sonorous voice which belongs to the indiscreet and quarrelsome. His dress was perfect. Ethel could find no fault in it, except the monocle which he did not use once during the evening, and which she therefore decided was a quite idle and unhandsome adjunct.

One feature of his character was definite—he was a home-loving man. He liked the society of women with whom he could be familiar, and he preferred the company of books and music to fashionable social functions. This pleasant habit of domesticity was illustrated during the evening by an accidental incident—a noisy, mechanical street organ stopped before the windows, and in a blatant manner began its performance. Conversation was paralyzed by the intrusion and when it was removed Judge Rawdon said: "What a democratic, leveling, aggressive thing music is! It insists on being heard. It is always in the way, it thrusts itself upon you, whether you want it or not. Now art is different. You go to see pictures when you wish to."

Mostyn did not notice the criticism on music itself, but added in a soft, disapproving way: "That man has no music in him. Do you know that was one of Mendelssohn's delicious dreams. This is how it should have been rendered," and he went impulsively to the piano and then the sweet

Amelia E. Barr

monotonous cadences and melodious reveries slipped from his long white fingers till the whole room was permeated with a delicious sense of moonlit solitude and conversation was stilled in its languor. The young man had played his own dismissal, but it was an effective one, and he complimented himself on his readiness to seize opportunities for display, and on his genius in satisfying them.

"I think I astonished them a little," he mused, "and I wonder what that pretty, cousin of mine thought of the music and the musician. I fancy we shall be good friends; she is proud— that is no fault; and she has very decided opinions—which might be a great fault; but I think I rather astonished them."

To such reflections he stepped rather pompously down the avenue, not at all influenced by any premonition that his satisfactory feelings might be imperfectly shared. Yet silence was the first result of his departure. Judge Rawdon took out his pocketbook and began to study its entries. Ruth Bayard rose and closed the piano. Ethel lifted a magazine, while it was Madam who finally asked in an impatient tone:

"What do you think of Frederick? I suppose, Edward, you have an opinion. Isn't he a very clever man?"

"I should not wonder if he were, mother, clever to a fault."

"I never heard a young man talk better."

"He talked a great deal, but then, you know, he was not on his oath."

"I'll warrant every word he said."

"Your warrant is fine surety, mother, but I am not bound to believe all I hear. You women can please yourselves."

And with these words he left the women to find out, if they could, what manner of man their newly-found kinsman might be.

* * * * * * *

CHAPTER III

ONE of the most comfortable things about Frederick Mostyn was his almost boyish delight in the new life which New York opened to him. Every phase of it was so fresh, so unusual, that his Yorkshire existence at Mostyn Hall gave him no precedents and no experiences by which to measure events. The simplest things were surprising or interesting. He was never weary of taking those exciting "lifts" to the top of twenty-three story buildings and admiring the wonderful views such altitudes gave him. He did not perhaps comprehend how much he was influenced by the friction of two million wills and interests; did not realize how they evoked an electric condition that got behind the foreground of existence and stirred something more at the roots of his being than any previous experience had ever done. And this feeling was especially entrancing when he saw the great city and majestic river lying at his feet in the white, uncanny light of electricity, all its color gone, its breath cold, its life strangely remote and quiet, men moving like shadows, and sounds hollow and faint and far off, as if they came from a distant world. It gave him a sense of dreamland quite as much as that of reality. The Yorkshire moors and words grew dull and dreary in his memory; even the thought of the hunting field could not lure his desire. New York was full of marvelous novelties; its daily routine, even in the hotel and on the streets, gripped his heart and his imagination; and he confessed to himself that New York was life at first hand; fresh drawn, its very foam sparkling and intoxicating. He walked from the Park to the Battery and examined all that caught his eye. He had a history of the city and sought out every historical site; he even went over to Weehawken, and did his best to locate the spot where Burr and Hamilton fought. He admired Hamilton, but after reading all about the two men, gave his sympathy to Burr, "a clever, unlucky little chap," he said. "Why do clever men hate each other?" and then he smiled queerly as he remembered political enemies of great men in his own day and his own country; and concluded that "it was their nature to do so."

But in these outside enthusiasms he did not forget his personal relations. It took him but a few days to domesticate himself in both the Rawdon houses. When the weather drove him off the streets, he found a pleasant refuge either with Madam or with Ethel and Miss Bayard. Ethel he saw less frequently than he liked; she was nearly always with Dora Denning, but with Ruth Bayard he contracted a very pleasant friendship. He told her all his adventures and found her more sympathetic than Madam ever pretended to be. Madam thought him provincial in his tastes, and was better pleased to hear that he had a visiting entry at two good clubs, and had hired a motor ear, and was learning how to manage it. Then she told herself that if he was good to her, she would buy him one to be proud of before he returned to Yorkshire.

It was at the Elite Club Bryce Denning first saw him. He came in with Shaw McLaren, a young man whose acquaintance was considered as most definitely satisfactory. Vainly Bryce Denning had striven to obtain any notice whatever from McLaren, whose exclusiveness was proverbial. Who then was this stranger he appeared so anxious to entertain? His look of supreme satisfaction, his high-bred air, and peculiar intonation quickly satisfied Bryce as to his nationality.

"English, of course," he reflected, "and probably one of the aristocrats that Shaw meets at his recently ennobled sister's place. He is forever bragging about them. I must find out who Shaw's last British lion is," and just as he arrived at this decision the person appeared who could satisfy him.

"That man!" was the reply to the inevitable question—"why, he is some relative of the old lady Rawdon. He is staying at the Holland House, but spends his time with the Rawdons, old and young; the young one is a beauty, you know."

"Do you think so? She is a good deal at our house. I suppose the fellow has some pretentions. Judge Rawdon will be a man hard to satisfy with a son-in-law."

"I fancy his daughter will take that subject in her own hand. She looks like a girl of spirit; and this man is not as handsome as most Englishmen."

"Not if you judge him by bulk, but women want more than mere bulk; he has an air of breeding you can't mistake, and he looks clever."

"His name is Mostyn. I have heard him spoken of. Would you like to know him?"

"I could live without that honor"—then Bryce turned the conversation upon a recent horse sale, and a few moments later was sauntering up the avenue. He was now resolved to make up his quarrel with Dora. Through Dora he could manage to meet Mostyn socially, and he smiled in anticipation of that proud moment when he should parade in his own friendly leash McLaren's new British lion. Besides, the introduction to Mr. Mostyn might, if judiciously managed, promote his own acquaintance with Shaw McLaren, a sequence to be much desired; an end he had persistently looked for.

He went straight to his sister's apartments and touched the bell quite gently. Her maid opened the door and looked annoyed and uncertain. She knew all about the cruelly wicked opposition of Miss Denning's brother to that nice young man, Basil Stanhope; and also the general attitude of the Denning household, which was a comprehensive disapproval of all that Mr. Bryce said and did.

Dora had, however, talked all her anger away; she wished now to be friends with her brother. She knew that his absence from her wedding would cause unpleasant notice, and she had other reasons, purely selfish, all emphasizing the advantages of a reconciliation. So she went to meet Bryce with a pretty, pathetic air of injury patiently endured, and when Bryce put out his hands and said, "Forgive me, Dodo! I cannot bear your anger any longer!" she was quite ready for the next act, which was to lay her pretty head on his shoulder and murmur, "I am not angry, Bryce—I am grieved, dear."

"I know, Dodo—forgive me! It was all my fault. I think I was jealous of you; it was hard to find that you loved a stranger better than you loved me. Kiss me, and be my own sweet, beautiful sister again. I shall try to like all the people you like—for your sake, you know."

Then Dora was charming. She sat and talked and planned and told him all that had been done and all that was yet to do. And Bryce never once named either Ethel or Mr. Mostyn. He knew Dora was a shrewd little woman, and that he would have to be very careful in introducing the subject of Mr. Mostyn, or else she would be sure to reach the central truth of his submission to her. But, somehow, things happen for those who are content to leave their desires to contingencies and accidentals. The next morning he breakfasted with the

Amelia E. Barr

family and felt himself repaid for his concession to Dora by the evident pleasure their renewed affection gave his father and mother; and though the elder Denning made no remark in the renewed family solidarity, Bryce anticipated many little favors and accommodations from his father's satisfaction.

After breakfast he sat down, lit his cigar and waited. Both his mother and Dora had much to tell him, and he listened, and gave them such excellent advice that they were compelled to regret the arrangements already made had lacked the benefit of his counsels.

"But you had Ethel Rawdon," he said. "I thought she was everybody rolled into one."

"Oh, Ethel doesn't know as much as she thinks she does," said Mrs. Denning. "I don't agree with lots of things she advises."

"Then take my advice, mother."

"Oh, Bryce, it is the best of all."

"Bryce does not know about dress and such things, mother. Ethel finds out what she does not know. Bryce cannot go to modistes and milliners with me."

"Well, Ethel does not pay as much attention as she might— she is always going somewhere or other with that Englishman, that she says is a relative—for my part, I doubt it."

"Oh, mother!"

"Girls will say anything, Dora, to hide a love affair. Why does she never bring him here to call?"

"Because I asked her not. I do not want to make new friends, especially English ones, now. I am so busy all day, and of course my evenings belong to Basil."

"Yes, and there is no one to talk to me. Ethel and the Englishman would pass an hour or two very nicely, and your father is very fond of foreigners. I think you ought to ask Ethel to introduce him to us; then we could have a little dinner for him and invite him to our opera box—don't you agree with me, Bryce?"

"If Dora does. Of course, at this time, Dora's wishes and engagements are the most important. I have seen the young man at the club with Shaw McLaren and about town with Judge Rawdon and others. He seems a nice little fellow. Jack Lacy wanted to introduce me to him yesterday, but I told him I could live without the honor. Of course, if Dora feels like having him here that is a very different matter. He is certainly distinguished looking, and would give an air to the wedding."

"Is he handsome, Bryce?"

"Yes—and no. Women would rave about him; men would think him finical and dandified. He looks as if he were the happiest fellow in the world—in fact, he looked to me so provokingly happy that I disliked him; but now that Dodo is my little sister again, I can be happy enough to envy no one."

Then Dora slipped her hand into her brother's hand, and Bryce knew that he might take his way to his little office in William Street, the advent of Mr. Mostyn into his life being now as certain as anything in this questionable, fluctuating world could be. As he was sauntering down the avenue he met Ethel and he turned and walked back with her to the Denning house. He was so good-natured and so good-humored that Ethel could not avoid an inquisitive look at the usually glum young man, and he caught it with a laugh and said, "I suppose you wonder what is the matter with me, Miss Rawdon?"

"You look more than usually happy. If I suppose you have found a wife or a fortune, shall I be wrong?"

"You come near the truth; I have found a sister. Do you know I am very fond of Dora and we have made up our quarrel?"

Then Ethel looked at him again. She did not believe him. She was sure that Dora was not the only evoker of the unbounded satisfaction in Bryce Denning's face and manner. But she let the reason pass; she had no likely arguments to use against it. And that day Mrs. Denning, with a slight air of injury, opened the subject of Mr. Mostyn's introduction to them. She thought Ethel had hardly treated the Dennings fairly. Everyone was wondering they had not met him. Of course, she knew they were not aristocrats and she supposed Ethel was ashamed of them, but, for her part, she thought they were as good as most people, and if it came to money, they could put down dollar for dollar with any multi-millionaire in America, or England either, for that matter.

When the reproach took this tone there seemed to be only one thing for Ethel to say or to do; but that one thing was exactly what she did not say or do. She took up Mrs. Denning's reproach and complained that "her relative and friend had been purposely and definitely ignored. Dora had told her plainly she did not wish to make Mr. Mostyn's acquaintance; and, in accord with this feeling, no one in the Denning family had called on Mr. Mostyn, or shown him the least courtesy. She thought the whole Rawdon family had the best of reasons for feeling hurt at the neglect."

This view of the case had not entered Mrs. Denning's mind. She was quickly sorry and apologetic for Dora's selfishness and her own thoughtlessness, and Ethel was not difficult to pacify. There was then no duty so imperative as the arrangement of a little dinner for Mr. Mostyn. "We will make it quite a family affair," said Mrs. Denning, "then we can go to the opera afterwards. Shall I call on Mr. Mostyn at the Holland House?" she asked anxiously.

"I will ask Bryce to call," said Dora. "Bryce will do anything to please me now, mother."

In this way, Bryce Denning's desires were all arranged for him, and that evening Dora made her request. Bryce heard it with a pronounced pout of his lips, but finally told Dora she was "irresistible," and as his time for pleasing her was nearly out, he would even call on the Englishman at her request.

"Mind!" he added, "I think he is as proud as Lucifer, and I may get nothing for my civility but the excuse of a previous engagement."

But Bryce Denning expected much more than this, and he got all that he expected. The young men had a common ground to meet on, and they quickly became as intimate as ever Frederick Mostyn permitted himself to be with a stranger. Bryce could hardly help catching enthusiasm from Mostyn on the subject of New York, and he was able to show his new acquaintance phases of life in the marvelous city which were of the greatest interest to the inquisitive Yorkshire squire—Chinese theaters and opium dives; German, Italian, Spanish, Jewish, French cities sheltering themselves within the great arms of the great American city; queer restaurants, where he could eat of the national dishes of every civilized country under the sun; places of amusement, legal and illegal, and the vast under side of the

Amelia E. Barr

evident life—all the uncared for toiling of the thousands who work through the midnight hours. In these excursions the young men became in a way familiar, though neither of them ever told the other the real feelings of their hearts or the real aim of their lives.

The proposed dinner took place ten days after its suggestion. There was nothing remarkable in the function itself; all millionaires have the same delicacies and the same wines, and serve these things with precisely the same ceremonies. And, as a general thing, the company follow rigidly ordained laws of conversation. Stories about public people, remarks about the weather and the opera, are in order; but original ideas or decided opinions are unpardonable social errors. Yet even these commonplace events may contain some element that shall unexpectedly cut a life in two, and so change its aims and desires as to virtually create a new character. It was Frederick Mostyn who in this instance underwent this great personal change; a change totally unexpected and for which he was absolutely unprepared. For the people gathered in Mrs. Denning's drawing-room were mostly known to him, and the exceptions did not appear to possess any remarkable traits, except Basil Stanhope, who stood thoughtfully at a window, his pale, lofty beauty wearing an air of expectation. Mostyn decided that he was naturally impatient for the presence of his fiancee, whose delayed entrance he perceived was also annoying Ethel. Then there was a slight movement, a sudden silence, and Mostyn saw Stanhope's face flush and turn magically radiant. Mechanically he followed his movement and the next moment his eyes met Fate, and Love slipped in between. Dora was there, a fairy-like vision in pale amber draperies, softened with silk lace. Diamonds were in her wonderfully waved hair and round her fair white neck. They clasped her belt and adorned the instep of her little amber silk slippers. She held a yellow rose in her hand, and yellow rosebuds lay among the lace at her bosom, and

Mostyn, stupefied by her undreamed-of loveliness, saw golden emanations from the clear pallor of her face. He felt for a moment or two as if he should certainly faint; only by a miracle of stubborn will did he drag his consciousness from that golden-tinted, sparkling haze of beauty which had smitten him like an enchantment. Then the girl was looking at him with her soft, dark, gazelle eyes; she was even speaking to him, but what she said, or what reply he made, he could never by any means remember. Miss Bayard was to be his companion, and with some effort and a few indistinct words he gave her his arm. She asked if he was ill, and when a shake of the head answered the query, she covered the few minutes of his disconcertion with her conversation. He looked at her gratefully and gathered his personality together. For Love had come to him like a two-edged sword, dividing the flesh and the spirit, and he longed to cry aloud and relieve the sweet torture of the possession.

Reaction, however, came quickly, and with it a wonderful access of all his powers. The sweet, strong wine of Love went to his brain like celestial nectar. All the witty, amusing things he had ever heard came trooping into his memory, and the dinner was long delayed by his fine humor, his pleasant anecdotes, and the laughing thoughts which others caught up and illustrated in their own way.

It was a feast full of good things, but its spirit was not able to bear transition. The company scattered quickly when it was over to the opera or theater or to the rest of a quiet evening at home, for at the end enthusiasm of any kind has a chilling effect on the feelings. None of the party understood this result, and yet all were, in their way, affected by the sudden fall of mental temperature. Mr. Denning went to his library and took out his private ledger, a penitential sort of reading which he relished after moods of any kind of enjoyment. Mrs. Denning selected Ethel Rawdon for her text of disillusion. She "thought Ethel had been a little jealous of Dora's dress," and Dora said, "It was one of her surprises, and Ethel thought she ought to know everything." "You are too obedient to Ethel," continued Mrs. Denning and Dora looked with a charming demureness at her lover, and said, "She had to be obedient to some one wiser than herself," and so slipped her hand into Basil's hand. And he understood the promise, and with a look of passionate affection raised the little jeweled pledge and kissed it.

Perhaps no one was more affected by this chill, critical after-hour than Miss Bayard and Ethel. Mostyn accompanied them home, but he was depressed, and his courtesy had the air of an obligation. He said he had a sudden headache, and was not sorry when the ladies bid him "good night" on the threshold. Indeed, he felt that he must have refused any invitation to lengthen out the hours with them or anybody. He wanted one thing, and he wanted that with all his soul— solitude, that he might fill it with images of Dora, and with passionate promises that either by fair means or by foul, by right or by wrong, he would win the bewitching woman for his wife.

CHAPTER IV

"WHAT do you think of the evening, Aunt Ruth?" Ethel was in her aunt's room, comfortably wrapped in a pink kimono, when she asked this question.

"What do you think of it, Ethel?"

"I am not sure."

"The dinner was well served."

"Yes. Who was the little dark man you talked with, aunt?"

"He was a Mr. Marriot, a banker, and a friend of Bryce Denning's. He is a fresh addition to society, I think. He had the word 'gold' always on his lips; and he believes in it as good men believe in God. The general conversation annoyed him; he could not understand men being entertained by it."

"They were, though, for once Jamie Sayer forgot to talk about his pictures."

"Is that the name of your escort?"

"Yes."

Amelia E. Barr

"And is he an artist?"

"A second-rate one. He is painting Dora's picture, and is a great favorite of Mrs. Denning's."

"A strange, wild-looking man. When I saw him first he was lying, dislocated, over his ottoman rather than sitting on it."

"Oh, that is a part of his affectations. He is really a childish, self-conscious creature, with a very decided dash of vulgarity. He only tries to look strange and wild, and he would be delighted if he knew you had thought him so."

"I was glad to see Claudine Jeffrys. How slim and graceful she is! And, pray, who is that Miss Ullman?"

"A very rich woman. She has Bryce under consideration. Many other men have been in the same position, for she is sure they all want her money and not her. Perhaps she is right. I saw you talking to her, aunt."

"For a short time. I did not enjoy her company. She is so mercilessly realistic, she takes all the color out of life. Everything about her, even her speech, is sharp-lined as the edge of a knife. She could make Bryce's life very miserable."

"Perhaps it might turn out the other way. Bryce Denning has capacities in the same line. How far apart, how far above every man there, stood Basil Stanhope!"

"He is strikingly handsome and graceful, and I am sure that his luminous serenity does not arise from apathy. I should say he was a man of very strong and tender feelings."

"And he gives all the strength and tenderness of his feelings to Dora. Men are strange creatures."

"Who directed Dora's dress this evening?"

"Herself or her maid. I had nothing to do with it. The effect was stunning."

"Fred thought so. In fact, Fred Hostyn—"

"Fell in love with her."

"Exactly. 'Fell,' that is the word—fell prostrate. Usually the lover of to-day walks very timidly and carefully into the condition, step by step, and calculating every step before he takes it. Fred plunged headlong into the whirling vortex. I am very sorry. It is a catastrophe."

"I never witnessed the accident before. I have heard of men getting wounds and falls, and developing new faculties in consequence, but we saw the phenomenon take place this evening."

"Love, if it be love, is known in a moment. man who never saw the sun before would know it was the sun. In Fred's case it was an instantaneous, impetuous passion, flaming up at the sight of such unexpected beauty—a passion that will probably fade as rapidly as it rose."

"Fred is not that kind of a man, aunt. He does not like every one and everything, but whoever or whatever he does like becomes a lasting part of his life. Even the old chairs and tables at Mostyn are held as sacred objects by him, though I have no doubt an American girl would trundle them off to the garret. It is the same with the people. He actually regards the Rawdons as belonging in some way to the Mostyns; and I do not believe he has ever been in love before."

Amelia E. Barr

"Nonsense!"

"He was so surprised by the attack. If it had been the tenth or twentieth time he would have taken it more philosophically; besides, if he had ever loved any woman, he would have gone on loving her, and we should have known all about her perfections by this time."

"Dora is nearly a married woman, and Mostyn knows it."

"Nearly may make all the difference. When Dora is married he will be compelled to accept the inevitable and make the best of it."

"When Dora is married he will idealize her, and assure himself that her marriage is the tragedy of both their lives."

"Dora will give him no reason to suppose such a thing. I am sure she will not. She is too much in love with Mr. Stanhope to notice any other lover."

"You are mistaken, Ethel. Swiftly as Fred was vanquished she noticed it, and many times—once even while leaning on Mr. Stanhope's arm—she turned the arrow in the heart wound with sweet little glances and smiles, and pretty appeals to the blind adoration of her new lover. It was, to me, a humiliating spectacle. How could she do it?"

"I am sure Dora meant no wrong. It is so natural for a lovely girl to show off a little. She will marry and forget Fred Mostyn lives."

"And Fred will forget?"

"Fred will not forget."

"Then I shall be very sorry for your father and grandmother."

"What have they to do with Fred marrying?"

"A great deal. Fred has been so familiar and homely the last two or three weeks, that they have come to look upon him as a future member of the family. It has been 'Cousin Ethel' and 'Aunt Ruth' and even 'grandmother' and 'Cousin Fred,' and no objections have been made to the use of such personal terms. I think your father hopes for a closer tie between you and Fred Mostyn than cousinship."

"Whatever might have been is over. Do you imagine I could consent to be the secondary deity, to come after Dora—Dora of all the girls I have ever known? The idea is an insult to my heart and my intelligence. Nothing on earth could make me submit to such an indignity."

"I do not suppose, Ethel, that any wife is the first object of her husband's love."

"At least they tell her she is so, swear it an inch deep; and no woman is fool enough to look beyond that oath, but when she is sure that she is a second best! AH! That is not a position I will ever take in any man's heart knowingly."

"Of course, Fred Mostyn will have to marry."

"Of course, he will make a duty of the event. The line of Mostyns must be continued. England might go to ruin if the Mostyns perished off the English earth; but, Aunt Ruth, I count myself worthy of a better fate than to become a mere branch in the genealogical tree of the Mostyns. And that is all Fred Mostyn's wife will ever be to him, unless he marries Dora."

Amelia E. Barr

"But that very supposition implies tragedy, and it is most unlikely."

"Yes, for Dora is a good little thing. She has never been familiar with vice. She has even a horror of poor women divorced from impossible husbands. She believes her marriage will be watched by the angels, and recorded in heaven. Basil has instructed her to regard marriage as a holy sacrament, and I am sure he does the same."

"Then why should we forecast evil to their names? As for Cousin Fred, I dare say he is comfortably asleep."

"I am sure he is not. I believe he is smoking and calling himself names for not having come to New York last May, when father first invited him. Had he done so things might have been different."

"Yes, they might. When Good Fortune calls, and the called 'will not when they may,' then, 'when they will' Good Fortune has become Misfortune. Welcome a pleasure or a gain at once, or don't answer it at all. It was on this rock, Ethel, the bark that carried my love went to pieces. I know; yes, I know!"

"My dear aunt!"

"It is all right now, dear; but things might have been that are not. As to Dora, I think she may be trusted with Basil Stanhope. He is one of the best and handsomest men I ever saw, and he has now rights in Dora's love no one can tamper with. Mostyn is an honorable man."

"All right, but—

"Love will venture in,

Where he daurna well be seen;
O Love will venture in,
Where Wisdom once has been—

and then, aunt, what then?"

PART SECOND

PLAYING WITH FIRE

CHAPTER V

THE next day after lunch Ethel said she was going to walk down to Gramercy Park and spend an hour or two with her grandmother, and "Will you send the carriage for me at five o'clock?" she asked.

"Your father has ordered the carriage to be at the Holland House at five o'clock. It can call for you first, and then go to the Holland House. But do not keep your father waiting. If he is not at the entrance give your card to the outside porter; he will have it sent up to Fred's apartments."

"Then father is calling on Fred? What for? Is he sick?"

"Oh, no, business of some kind. I hope you will have a pleasant walk."

"There is no doubt of it."

Indeed, she was radiant with its exhilaration when she reached Gramercy Park. As she ran up the steps of the big, old-fashioned house she saw Madam at the window picking up some dropped stitches in her knitting. Madam saw her at the same moment, and the old face and the young face both alike kindled with love, as well as with happy anticipation of coveted intercourse.

"I am so glad to see you, darling Granny. I could not wait until to-morrow."

"And why should you, child? I have been watching for you all morning. I want to hear about the Denning dinner. I suppose you went?"

"Yes, we went; we had to. Dinners in strange houses are a common calamity; I can't expect to be spared what everyone has to endure."

"Don't be affected, Ethel. You like going out to dinner. Of course, you do! It is only natural, considering."

"I don't, Granny. I like dances and theaters and operas, but I don't like dinners. However, the Denning dinner was a grand exception. It gave me and the others a sensation."

"I expected that."

"It was beautifully ordered. Major-domo Parkinson saw to that. If he had arranged it for his late employer, the Duke of Richmond, it could not have been finer. There was not a break anywhere."

"How many were present?"

"Just a dozen."

"Mr. Denning and Bryce, of course. Who were the others?"

"Mr. Stanhope, of course. Granny, he wore his clerical dress. It made him look so remarkable."

"He did right. A clergyman ought to look different from other men. I do not believe Basil Stanhope, having assumed

Amelia E. Barr

the dress of a servant of God, would put it off one hour for any social exigency. Why should he? It is a grander attire than any military or naval uniform, and no court dress is comparable, for it is the court dress of the King of kings."

"All right, dear Granny; you always make things clear to me, yet I meet lots of clergymen in evening dress."

"Then they ought not to be clergymen. They ought not to wear coats in which they can hold any kind of opinions. Who was your companion?"

"Jamie Sayer."

"I never heard of the man."

"He is an artist, and is painting Dora's likeness. He is getting on now, but in the past, like all artists, he has suffered a deal."

"God's will be done. Let them suffer. It is good for genius to suffer. Is he in love with you?"

"Gracious, Granny! His head is so full of pictures that no woman could find room there, and if one did, the next new picture would crowd her out."

"End that story, it is long enough."

"Do you know Miss Ullman?"

"I have heard of her. Who has not?"

"She has Bryce Denning on trial now. If he marries her I shall pity him."

"Pity him! Not I, indeed! He would have his just reward. Like to like, and Amen to it."

"Then there was Claudine Jeffrys, looking quite ethereal, but very lovely."

"I know. Her lover was killed in Cuba, and she has been the type of faithful grief ever since. She looks it and dresses it to perfection."

"And feels it?"

"Perhaps she does. I am not skilled in the feelings of pensive, heart-broken maidens. But her case is a very common one. Lovers are nowhere against husbands, yet how many thousands of good women lose their husbands every year? If they are poor, they have to hide their grief and work for themselves and their families; if they are rich, very few people believe that they are really sorry to be widows. Are any poor creatures more jeered at than widows? No man believes they are grieving for the loss of their husbands. Then why should they all sympathize with Claudine about the loss of a lover?"

"Perhaps lovers are nicer than husbands."

"Pretty much all alike. I have known a few good husbands. Your grandfather was one, your father another. But you have said nothing about Fred. Did he look handsome? Did he make a sensation? Was he a cousin to be proud of?"

"Indeed, Granny, Fred was the whole party. He is not naturally handsome, but he has distinction, and he was well-dressed. And I never heard anyone talk as he did. He told the most delightful stories, he was full of mimicry and wit, and said things that brought everyone into the merry talk; and I am sure he charmed and astonished the whole party. Mr. Denning asked me quietly afterwards 'what university he was educated at.' I think he took it all as education, and had some wild ideas of finishing Bryce in a similar manner."

Madam was radiant. "I told you so," she said proudly. "The Mostyns have intellect as well as land. There are no stupid Mostyns. I hope you asked him to play. I think his way of handling a piano would have taught them a few things Russians and Poles know nothing about. Poor things! How can they have any feelings left?"

"There was no piano in the room, Granny, and the company separated very soon after dinner."

"Somehow you ought to have managed it, Ethel." Then with a touch of anxiety, "I hope all this cleverness was natural—I mean, I hope it wasn't champagne. You know, Ethel, we think as we drink, and Fred isn't used to those frisky wines. Mostyn cellars are full of old sherry and claret, and Fred's father was always against frothing, sparkling wines."

"Granny, it was all Fred. Wine had nothing to do with it, but a certain woman had; in fact, she was the inspirer, and Fred fell fifty fathoms deep in love with her the very moment she entered the room. He heard not, felt not, thought not, so struck with love was he. Ruth got him to a window for a few moments and so hid his emotion until he could get himself together."

"Oh, what a tale! What a cobweb tale! I don't believe a word of it," and she laughed merrily.

"'Tis true as gospel, Granny."

"Name her, then. Who was the woman?"

"Dora."

"It is beyond belief, above belief, out of all reason. It cannot be, and it shall not be, and if you are making up a story to tease me, Ethel Rawdon—"

"Grandmother, let me tell you just how it came about. We were all in the room waiting for Dora, and she suddenly entered. She was dressed in soft amber silk from head to feet; diamonds were in her black hair, and on the bands across her shoulders, on her corsage, on her belt, her hands, and even her slippers. Under the electric lights she looked as if she was in a golden aura, scintillating with stars. She took Fred's breath away. He was talking to Ruth, and he could not finish the word he was saying. Ruth thought he was going to faint—"

"Don't tell me such nonsense."

"Well, grandmother, this nonsense is truth. As I said before, Ruth took him aside until he got control of himself; then, as he was Dora's escort, he had to go to her. Ruth introduced them, and as she raised her soft, black eyes to his, and put her hand on his arm, something happened again, but this time it was like possession. He was the courtier in a moment, his eyes flashed back her glances, he gave her smile for smile, and then when they were seated side by side he became inspired and talked as I have told you. It is the truth, grandmother."

"Well, there are many different kinds of fools, but Fred Mostyn is the worst I ever heard tell of. Does he not know that the girl is engaged?"

"Knows it as well as I do."

"None of our family were ever fools before, and I hope Fred will come round quickly. Do you think Dora noticed the impression she made?"

"Yes, Aunt Ruth noticed Dora; and Ruth says Dora 'turned the arrow in the heart wound' all the evening."

"What rubbish you are talking! Say in good English what you mean."

"She tried every moment they, were together to make him more and more in love with her."

"What is her intention? A girl doesn't carry on that way for nothing."

"I do not know. Dora has got beyond me lately. And, grandmother, I am not troubling about the event as it regards Dora or Fred or Basil Stanhope, but as it regards Ethel."

"What have you to do with it?"

"That is just what I want to have clearly understood. Aunt Ruth told me that father and you would be disappointed if I did not marry Fred."

"Well?"

"I am sorry to disappoint you, but I never shall marry Fred Mostyn. Never!"

"I rather think you will have to settle that question with your father, Ethel."

"No. I have settled it with myself. The man has given to Dora all the love that he has to give. I will have a man's whole heart, and not fragments and finger-ends of it."

"To be sure, that is right. But I can't say much, Ethel, when I only know one side of the case, can I? I must wait and hear what Fred has to say. But I like your spirit and your way of bringing what is wrong straight up to question. You are a bit Yorkshire yet, whatever you think gets quick to your tongue, and then out it comes. Good girl, your heart is on your lips."

They talked the afternoon away on this subject, but Madam's last words were not only advisory, they were in a great measure sympathetic. "Be straight with yourself, Ethel," she said, "then Fred Mostyn can do as he likes; you will be all right."

She accepted the counsel with a kiss, and then drove to the Holland House for her father. He was not waiting, as Ruth had supposed he would be, but then she was five minutes too soon. She sent up her card, and then let her eyes fall upon a wretched beggar man who was trying to play a violin, but was unable by reason of hunger and cold. He looked as if he was dying, and she was moved with a great pity, and longed for her father to come and give some help. While she was anxiously watching, a young man was also struck with the suffering on the violinist's face. He spoke a few words to him, and taking the violin, drew from it such strains of melody, that in a few moments a crowd had gathered within the hotel and before it. First there was silence, then a shout of delight; and when it ceased the player's voice thrilled every heart to passionate patriotism, as he sang with magnificent power and feeling—

There is not a spot on this wide-peopled earth
So dear to our heart as the Land of our Birth, etc.

A tumult of hearty applause followed, and then he cried,

Amelia E. Barr

"Gentlemen, this old man fought for the land of our birth. He is dying of hunger," and into the old man's hat he dropped a bill and then handed it round to millionaire and workingman alike. Ethel's purse was in her hand. As he passed along the curb at which her carriage stood, he looked at her eager face, and with a smile held out the battered hat. She, also smiling, dropped her purse into it. In a few moments the hat was nearly full; the old man and the money were confided to the care of an hotel officer, the stream of traffic and pleasure went on its usual way, and the musician disappeared.

All that evening the conversation turned constantly to this event. Mostyn was sure he was a member of some operatic troupe. "Voices of such rare compass and exceptional training were not to be found among non-professional people," he said, and Judge Rawdon was of his opinion.

"His voice will haunt me for many days," he said. "Those two lines, for instance—

'Tis the home of our childhood, that beautiful spot
Which memory retains when all else is forgot.

The melody was wonderful. I wish we could find out where he is singing. His voice, as I said, haunts my ear."

Ethel might have made the same remark, but she was silent. She had noticed the musician more closely than her father or Fred Mostyn, and when Ruth Bayard asked her if his personality was interesting, she was able to give a very clear description of the man.

"I do not believe he is a professional singer; he is too young," she answered. "I should think he was about twenty-five years old, tall, slender, and alert. He was fashionably dressed, as if he had been, or was going, to an afternoon reception. Above all things, I should say he was a gentleman."

Oh, why are our hearts so accessible to our eyes? Only a smiling glance had passed between Ethel and the Unknown, yet his image was prisoned behind the bars of her eyelids. On this day of days she had met Love on the crowded street, and he had

> "But touched his lute wherein was audible
> The certain secret thing he had to tell;
> Only their mirrored eyes met silently";

and a sweet trouble, a restless, pleasing curiosity, had filled her consciousness. Who was he? Where had he gone to? When should they meet again? Ah, she understood now how Emmeline Labiche had felt constrained to seek her lover from the snows of Canada to the moss-veiled oaks of Louisiana.

But her joyous, hopeful soul could not think of love and disappointment at the same moment. "I have seen him, and I shall see him again. We met by appointment. Destiny introduced us. Neither of us will forget, and somewhere, some day, I shall be waiting, and he will come."

Thus this daughter of sunshine and hope answered herself; and why not? All good things come to those who can wait in sweet tranquillity for them, and seldom does Fortune fail to bring love and heart's-ease upon the changeful stream of changeful days to those who trust her for them.

On the following morning, when the two girls entered the parlor, they found the Judge smoking there. He had already breakfasted, and looked over the three or four newspapers whose opinions he thought worthy of his consideration. They were lying in a state of confusion at his side, and Ethel

Amelia E. Barr

glanced at them curiously.

"Did any of the papers speak of the singing before the Holland House?" she asked.

"Yes. I think reporters must be ubiquitous. All my papers had some sort of a notice of the affair."

"What do they say?"

"One gave the bare circumstances of the case; another indulged in what was supposed to be humorous description; a third thought it might have been the result of a bet or dare; a fourth was of the opinion that conspiracy between the old beggar and the young man was not unlikely, and credited the exhibition as a cleverly original way of obtaining money. But all agreed in believing the singer to be a member of some opera company now in the city."

Ethel was indignant. "It was neither 'bet' nor 'dare' nor 'conspiracy,'" she said. "I saw the singer as he came walking rapidly down the avenue, and he looked as happy and careless as a boy whistling on a country lane. When his eyes fell on the old man he hesitated, just a moment, and then spoke to him. I am sure they were absolute strangers to each other."

"But how can you be sure of a thing like that, Ethel?"

"I don't know 'how,' Ruth, but all the same, I am sure. And as for it being a new way of begging, that is not correct. Not many years ago, one of the De Reszke brothers led a crippled soldier into a Paris cafe, and sang the starving man into comfort in twenty minutes."

"And the angelic Parepa Rosa did as much for a Mexican

woman, whom she found in the depths of sorrow and poverty—brought her lifelong comfort with a couple of her songs. Is it not likely, then, that the gallant knight of the Holland House is really a member of some opera company, that he knew of these examples and followed them?"

"It is not unlikely, Ruth, yet I do not believe that is the explanation."

"Well," said the Judge, throwing his cigarette into the fire, "if the singer had never heard of De Reszke and Parepa Rosa, we may suppose him a gentleman of such culture as to be familiar with the exquisite Greek legend of Phoebus Apollo—that story would be sufficient to inspire any man with his voice. Do you know it?"

Both girls answered with an enthusiastic entreaty for its recital, and the Judge went to the library and returned with a queer-looking little book, bound in marbled paper.

"It was my father's copy," he said, "an Oxford edition." And he turned the leaves with loving carefulness until he came to the incident. Then being a fine reader, the words fell from his lips in a stately measure better than music:

"After Troy fell there came to Argos a scarred soldier seeking alms. Not deigning to beg, he played upon a lyre; but the handling of arms had robbed him of his youthful power, and he stood by the portico hour after hour, and no one dropped him a lepton. Weary, hungry and thirsty, he leaned in despair against a pillar. A youth came to him and asked, 'Why not play on, Akeratos?" And Akeratos meekly answered, 'I am no longer skilled.' 'Then,' said the stranger, 'hire me thy lyre; here is a didrachmon. I will play, and thou shalt hold out thy cap and be dumb.' So the stranger took the lyre and swept the strings, and men heard, as it were, the

Amelia E. Barr

clashing of swords. And he sang the fall of Troy—how Hector perished, slain by Achilles, the rush of chariots, the ring of hoofs, the roar of flames—and as he sang the people stopped to listen, breathless and eager, with rapt, attentive ear. And when the singer ceased the soldier's cap was filled with coins, and the people begged for yet another song. Then he sang of Venus, till all men's hearts were softly stirred, and the air was purple and misty and full of the scent of roses. And in their joy men cast before Akeratos not coins only, but silver bracelets and rings, and gems and ornaments of gold, until the heap had to its utmost grown, making Akeratos rich in all men's sight. Then suddenly the singer stood in a blaze of light, and the men of Argos saw their god of song, Phoebus Apollo, rise in glory to the skies."

The girls were delighted; the Judge pleased both with his own rendering of the legend and the manifest appreciation with which it had been received. For a moment or two all felt the exquisite touch of the antique world, and Ethel said, in a tone of longing,

"I wish that I had been a Greek and lived in Argos."

"You would not have liked it as well as being an American and living in New York," said her father.

"And you would have been a pagan," added Ruth.

"They were such lovely pagans, Ruth, and they dreamed such beautiful dreams of life. Leave the book with me, father; I will take good care of it."

Then the Judge gave her the book, and with a sigh looked into the modern street. "I ought to be down at Bowling Green instead of reading Greek stories to you girls," he said rather brusquely. "I have a very important railway case on my mind, and Phoebus Apollo has nothing to do with it. Good morning. And, Ethel, do not deify the singer on the avenue. He will not turn out, like the singer by the portico, to be a god; be sure of that."

The door closed before she could answer, and both women remained silent a few minutes. Then Ethel went to the window, and Ruth asked if she was going to Dora's.

"Yes," was the answer, but without interest.

"You are tired with all this shopping and worry?"

"It is not only that I am tired, I am troubled about Fred Mostyn."

"Why?"

"I do not know why. It is only a vague unrest as yet. But one thing I know, I shall oppose anything like Fred making himself intimate with Dora."

"I think you will do wisely in that."

But in a week Ethel realized that in opposing a lover like Fred Mostyn she had a task beyond her ability. Fred had nothing to do as important in his opinion as the cultivation of his friendship with Dora Denning. He called it "friendship," but this misnomer deceived no one, not even Dora. And when Dora encouraged his attentions, how was Ethel to prevent them without some explanation which would give a sort of reality to what was as yet a nameless suspicion?

Yet every day the familiarity increased. He seemed to divine their engagements. If they went to their jeweler's, or to a bazaar, he was sure to stroll in after them. When they came out of the milliner's or modiste's, Fred was waiting. "He had secured a table at Sherry's; he had ordered lunch, and all was ready." It was too great an effort to resist his entreaty. Perhaps no one wished to do so. The girls were utterly tired and hungry, and the thought of one of Fred's lunches was very pleasant. Even if Basil Stanhope was with them, it appeared to be all the better. Fred always included Dora's lover with a charming courtesy; and, indeed, at such hours, was in his most delightful mood. Stanhope appeared to inspire him. His mentality when the clergyman was present took possession of every incident that came and went, and clothed it in wit and pleasantry. Dora's plighted lover honestly thought Dora's undeclared lover the cleverest and most delightful of men. And he had no opportunity of noting, as Ethel did, the difference in Fred's attitude when he was not present. Then Mostyn's merry mood became sentimental, and his words were charged with soft meanings and looks of adoration, and every tone and every movement made to express far more than the tongue would have dared to utter.

As this flirtation progressed—for on Dora's part it was only vanity and flirtation—Ethel grew more and more uneasy. She almost wished for some trifling overt act which would give her an excuse for warning Dora; and one day, after three weeks of such philandering, the opportunity came.

"I think you permit Fred Mostyn to take too much liberty with you, Dora," she said as soon as they were in Dora's parlor, and as she spoke she threw off her coat in a temper which effectively emphasized the words.

"I have been expecting this ill-nature, Ethel. You were cross all the time we were at lunch. You spoiled all our pleasure Pray, what have I been doing wrong with Fred Mostyn?"

"It was Fred who did wrong. His compliments to you were

outrageous. He has no right to say such things, and you have no right to listen to them."

"I am not to blame if he compliments me instead of you. He was simply polite, but then it was to the wrong person."

"Of course it was. Such politeness he had no right to offer you."

"It would have been quite proper if offered you, I suppose?"

"It would not. It would have been a great impertinence. I have given him neither claim nor privilege to address me as 'My lovely Ethel!' He called you many times 'My lovely Dora!' You are not his lovely Dora. When he put on your coat, he drew you closer than was proper; and I saw him take your hand and hold it in a clasp—not necessary."

"Why do you listen and watch? It is vulgar. You told me so yourself. And I am lovely. Basil says that as well as Fred. Do you want a man to lie and say I am ugly?"

"You are fencing the real question. He had no business to use the word 'my.' You are engaged to Basil Stanhope, not to Fred Mostyn."

"I am Basil's lovely fiancee; I am Fred's lovely friend."

"Oh! I hope Fred understands the difference."

"Of course he does. Some people are always thinking evil."

"I was thinking of Mr. Stanhope's rights."

"Thank you, Ethel; but I can take care of Mr. Stanhope's rights without your assistance. If you had said you were thinking of Ethel Rawdon's rights you would have been nearer the truth."

"Dora, I will not listen—"

"Oh, you shall listen to me! I know that you expected Fred to fall in love with you, but if he did not like to do so, am I to blame?" Ethel was resuming her coat at this point in the conversation, and Dora understood the proud silence with which the act was being accomplished. Then a score of good reasons for preventing such a definite quarrel flashed through her selfish little mind, and she threw her arms around Ethel and begged a thousand pardons for her rudeness. And Ethel had also reasons for avoiding dissension at this time. A break in their friendship now would bring Dora forward to explain, and Dora had a wonderful cleverness in presenting her own side of any question. Ethel shrunk from her innuendoes concerning Fred, and she knew that Basil would be made to consider her a meddling, jealous girl who willingly saw evil in Dora's guileless enjoyment of a clever man's company.

To be misunderstood, to be blamed and pitied, to be made a pedestal for Dora's superiority, was a situation not to be contemplated. It was better to look over Dora's rudeness in the flush of Dora's pretended sorrow for it. So they forgave each other, or said they did, and then Dora explained herself. She declared that she had not the least intention of any wrong. "You see, Ethel, what a fool the man is about me. Somebody says we ought to treat a fool according to his folly. That is all I was doing. I am sure Basil is so far above Fred Mostyn that I could never put them in comparison—and Basil knows it. He trusts me."

"Very well, Dora. If Basil knows it, and trusts you, I have no more to say. I am now sorry I named the subject."

"Never mind, we will forget that it was named. The fact is, Ethel, I want all the fun I can get now. When I am Basil's wife I shall have to be very sedate, and of course not even pretend to know if any other man admires me. Little lunches with Fred, theater and opera parties, and even dances will be over for me. Oh, dear, how much I am giving up for Basil! And sometimes I think he never realizes how dreadful it must be for me."

"You will have your lover all the time then. Surely his constant companionship will atone for all you relinquish."

"Take off your coat and hat, Ethel, and sit down comfortably. I don't know about Basil's constant companionship. Tete-a-tetes are tiresome affairs sometimes."

"Yes," replied Ethel, as she half-reluctantly removed her coat, "they were a bore undoubtedly even in Paradise. I wonder if Eve was tired of Adam's conversation, and if that made her listen to—the other party."

"I am so glad you mentioned that circumstance, Ethel. I shall remember it. Some day, no doubt, I shall have to remind Basil of the failure of Adam to satisfy Eve's idea of perfect companionship." And Dora put her pretty, jeweled hands up to her ears and laughed a low, musical laugh with a childish note of malice running through it.

This pseudo-reconciliation was not conducive to pleasant intercourse. After a short delay Ethel made an excuse for an early departure, and Dora accepted it without her usual remonstrance. The day had been one of continual friction, and Dora's irritable pettishness hard to bear, because it had now lost that childish unreason which had always induced Ethel's patience, for Dora had lately put away all her ignorant immaturities. She had become a person of importance, and

Amelia E. Barr

had realized the fact. The young ladies of St. Jude's had made a pet of their revered rector's love, and the elder ladies had also shown a marked interest in her. The Dennings' fine house was now talked about and visited. Men of high financial power respected Mr. Dan Denning, and advised the social recognition of his family; and Mrs. Denning was not now found more eccentric than many other of the new rich, who had been tolerated in the ranks of the older plutocrats. Even Bryce had made the standing he desired. He was seen with the richest and idlest young men, and was invited to the best houses. Those fashionable women who had marriageable daughters considered him not ineligible, and men temporarily hampered for cash knew that they could find smiling assistance for a consideration at Bryce's little office on William Street.

These and other points of reflection troubled Ethel, and she was glad the long trial was nearing its end, for she knew quite well the disagreement of that evening had done no good. Dora would certainly repeat their conversation, in her own way of interpreting it, to both Basil Stanhope and Fred Mostyn. More than likely both Bryce and Mrs. Denning would also hear how her innocent kindness had been misconstrued; and in each case she could imagine the conversation that took place, and the subsequent bestowal of pitying, scornful or angry feeling that would insensibly find its way to her consciousness without any bird of the air to carry it.

She felt, too, that reprisals of any kind were out of the question. They were not only impolitic, they were difficult. Her father had an aversion to Dora, and was likely to seize the first opportunity for requesting Ethel to drop the girl's acquaintance. Ruth also had urged her to withdraw from any active part in the wedding, strengthening her advice with the assurance that when a friendship began to decline it ought to be abandoned at once. There was only her grandmother to go to, and at first she did not find her at all interested in the trouble. She had just had a dispute with her milkman, was inclined to give him all her suspicions and all her angry words—"an impertinent, cheating creature," she said; and then Ethel had to hear the history of the month's cream and of the milkman's extortion, with the old lady's characteristic declaration:

"I told him plain what I thought of his ways, but I paid him every cent I owed him. Thank God, I am not unreasonable!"

Neither was she unreasonable when Ethel finally got her to listen to her own serious grievance with Dora.

"If you will have a woman for a friend, Ethel, you must put up with womanly ways; and it is best to keep your mouth shut concerning such ways. I hate to see you whimpering and whining about wrongs you have been cordially inviting for weeks and months and years."

"Grandmother!"

"Yes, you have been sowing thorns for yourself, and then you go unshod over them. I mean that Dora has this fine clergyman, and Fred Mostyn, and her brother, and mother, and father all on her side; all of them sure that Dora can do no wrong, all of them sure that Ethel, poor girl, must be mistaken, or prudish, or jealous, or envious."

"Oh, grandmother, you are too cruel,"

"Why didn't you have a few friends on your own side?"

"Father and Ruth never liked Dora. And Fred—I told you how Fred acted as soon as he saw her!"

"There was Royal Wheelock, James Clifton, or that handsome Dick Potter. Why didn't you ask them to join you at your lunches and dances? You ought to have pillared your own side. A girl without her beaux is always on the wrong side if the girl with beaux is against her."

"It was the great time of Dora's life. I wished her to have all the glory of it."

"All her own share—that was right. All of your share, also—that was as wrong as it could be."

"Clifton is yachting, Royal and I had a little misunderstanding, and Dick Potter is too effusive."

"But Dick's effusiveness would have been a good thing for Fred's effusiveness. Two men can't go on a complimentary ran-tan at the same table. They freeze one another out. That goes without saying. But Dora's indiscretions are none of your business while she is under her father's roof; and I don't know if she hadn't a friend in the world, if they would be your business. I have always been against people trying to do the work of THEM that are above us. We are told THEY seek and THEY save, and it's likely they will look after Dora in spite of her being so unknowing of herself as to marry a priest in a surplice, when a fool in motley would have been more like the thing."

"I don't want to quarrel with Dora. After all, I like her. We have been friends a long time."

"Well, then, don't make an enemy of her. One hundred friends are too few against one enemy. One hundred friends will wish you well, and one enemy will DO you ill. God love you, child! Take the world as you find it. Only God can make it any better. When is this blessed wedding to come off?"

"In two weeks. You got cards, did you not?"

"I believe I did. They don't matter. Let Dora and her flirtations alone, unless you set your own against them. Like cures like. If the priest sees nothing wrong—"

"He thinks all she does is perfect."

"I dare say. Priests are a soft lot, they'll believe anything. He's love-blind at present. Some day, like the prophet of Pethor,[1] he will get his eyes opened. As for Fred Mostyn, I shall have a good deal to say about him by and by, so I'll say nothing now."

[1] One of the Hebrew prophets.

"You promised, grandmother, not to talk to me any more about Fred."

"It was a very inconsiderate promise, a very irrational promise! I am sorry I made it—and I don't intend to keep it."

"Well, it takes two to hold a conversation, grandmother."

"To be sure it does. But if I talk to you, I hope to goodness you will have the decency to answer me. I wouldn't believe anything different." And she looked into Ethel's face with such a smiling confidence in her good will and obedience, that Ethel could only laugh and give her twenty kisses as she stood up to put on her hat and coat.

"You always get your way, Granny," she said; and the old lady, as she walked with her to the door, answered, "I have had my way for nearly eighty years, dearie, and I've found it a very good way. I'm not likely to change it now."

"And none of us want you to change it, dear. Granny's way is always a wise way." And she kissed her again ere she ran down the steps to her carriage. Yet as the old lady stepped slowly back to the parlor, she muttered, "Fred Mostyn is a fool! If he had any sense when he left England, he has lost it since he came here."

Of course nothing good came of this irritable interference. Meddling with the conscience of another person is a delicate and difficult affair, and Ruth had already warned Ethel of its certain futility. But the days were rapidly wearing away to the great day, for which so many other days had been wasted in fatiguing worry, and incredible extravagance of health and temper and money—and after it? There would certainly be a break in associations. Temptation would be removed, and Basil Stanhope, relieved for a time from all the duties of his office, would have continual opportunities for making eternally secure the affection of the woman he had chosen.

It was to be a white wedding, and for twenty hours previous to its celebration it seemed as if all the florists in New York were at work in the Denning house and in St. Jude's church. The sacred place was radiant with white lilies. White lilies everywhere; and the perfume would have been over-powering, had not the weather been so exquisite that open windows were possible and even pleasant. To the softest strains of music Dora entered leaning on her father's arm and her beauty and splendor evoked from the crowd present an involuntary, simultaneous stir of wonder and delight. She had hesitated many days between the simplicity of white chiffon and lilies of the valley, and the magnificence of brocaded satin in which a glittering thread of silver was interwoven. The satin had won the day, and the sunshine fell upon its beauty, as she knelt at the altar, like sunshine falling upon snow. It shone and gleamed and glistened as if it were an angel's robe; and this scintillating effect was much increased by the sparkling of the diamonds in her hair, and at her throat and waist and hands and feet. Nor was her brilliant youth affected by the overshadowing tulle usually so unbecoming. It veiled her from head to feet, and was held in place by a diamond coronal. All her eight maids, though lovely girls, looked wan and of the earth beside her. For her sake they had been content with the simplicity of chiffon and white lace hats, and she stood among them lustrous as some angelic being. Stanhope was entranced by her beauty, and no one on this day wondered at his infatuation or thought remarkable the ecstasy of reverent rapture with which he received the hand of his bride. His sense of the gift was ravishing. She was now his love, his wife forever, and when Ethel slipped forward to part and throw backward the concealing veil, he very gently restrained her, and with his own hands uncovered the blushing beauty, and kissed her there at the altar. Then amid a murmur and stir of delighted sympathy he took his wife upon his arm, and turned with her to the life they were to face together.

Two hours later all was a past dream. Bride and bridegroom had slipped quietly away, and the wedding guests had arrived at that rather noisy indifference which presages the end of an entertainment. Then flushed and tired with hurrying congratulations and good wishes that stumbled over each other, carriage after carriage departed; and Ethel and her companions went to Dora's parlor to rest awhile and discuss the event of the day. But Dora's parlor was in a state of confusion. It had, too, an air of loss, and felt like a gilded cage from which the bird had flown. They looked dismally at its discomfort and went downstairs. Men were removing the faded flowers or sitting at the abandoned table eating and drinking. Everywhere there was disorder and waste, and from the servants' quarter came a noisy sense of riotous feasting.

Amelia E. Barr

"Where is Mrs. Denning?" Ethel asked a footman who was gathering together the silver with the easy unconcern of a man whose ideas were rosy with champagne. He looked up with a provoking familiarity at the question, and sputtered out, "She's lying down crying and making a fuss. Miss Day is with her, soothing of her."

"Let us go home," said Ethel.

And so, weary with pleasure, and heart-heavy with feelings that had no longer any reason to exist, pale with fatigue, untidy with crush, their pretty white gowns sullied and passe, each went her way; in every heart a wonder whether the few hilarious hours of strange emotions were worth all they claimed as their right and due.

Ruth had gone home earlier, and Ethel found her resting in her room. "I am worn out, Ruth," was her first remark. "I am going to bed for three or four days. It was a dreadful ordeal."

"One to which you may have to submit."

"Certainly not. My marriage will be a religious ceremony, with half a dozen of my nearest relatives as witnesses."

"I noticed Fred slip away before Dora went. He looked ill."

"I dare say he is ill—and no wonder. Good night, Ruth. I am going to sleep. Tell father all about the wedding. I don't want to hear it named again—not as long as I live."

CHAPTER VI

THREE days passed and Ethel had regained her health and spirits, but Fred Mostyn had not called since the wedding. Ruth thought some inquiry ought to be made, and Judge Rawdon called at the Holland House. There he was told that Mr. Mostyn had not been well, and the young man's countenance painfully confessed the same thing.

"My dear Fred, why did you not send us word you were ill?" asked the Judge.

"I had fever, sir, and I feared it might be typhoid. Nothing of the kind, however. I shall be all right in a day or two."

The truth was far from typhoid, and Fred knew it. He had left the wedding breakfast because he had reached the limit of his endurance. Words, stinging as whips, burned like hot coals in his mouth, and he felt that he could not restrain them much longer. Hastening to his hotel, he locked himself in his rooms, and passed the night in a frenzy of passion. The very remembrance of the bridegroom's confident transport put murder in his heart—murder which he could only practice by his wishes, impotent to compass their desires.

"I wish the fellow shot! I wish him hanged! I would kill him twenty times in twenty different ways! And Dora! Dora!

Amelia E. Barr

Dora! What did she see in him? What could she see? Love her? He knows nothing of love—such love as tortures me." Backwards and forwards he paced the floor to such imprecations and ejaculations as welled up from the whirlpool of rage in his heart, hour following hour, till in the blackness of his misery he could no longer speak. His brain had become stupefied by the iteration of inevitable loss, and so refused any longer to voice a woe beyond remedy. Then he stood still and called will and reason to council him. "This way madness lies," he thought. "I must be quiet—I must sleep—I must forget."

But it was not until the third day that a dismal, sullen stillness succeeded the storm of rage and grief, and he awoke from a sleep of exhaustion feeling as if he were withered at his heart. He knew that life had to be taken up again, and that in all its farces he must play his part. At first the thought of Mostyn Hall presented itself as an asylum. It stood amid thick woods, and there were miles of wind-blown wolds and hills around it. He was lord and master there, no one could intrude upon his sorrow; he could nurse it in those lonely rooms to his heart's content. Every day, however, this gloomy resolution grew fainter, and one morning he awoke and laughed it to scorn.

"Frederick's himself again," he quoted, "and he must have been very far off himself when he thought of giving up or of running away. No, Fred Mostyn, you will stay here. 'Tis a country where the impossible does not exist, and the unlikely is sure to happen—a country where marriage is not for life or death, and where the roads to divorce are manifold and easy. There are a score of ways and means. I will stay and think them over; 'twill be odd if I cannot force Fate to change her mind."

A week after Dora's marriage he found himself able to walk

up the avenue to the Rawdon house; but he arrived there weary and wan enough to instantly win the sympathy of Ruth and Ethel, and he was immensely strengthened by the sense of home and kindred, and of genuine kindness to which he felt a sort of right. He asked Ruth if he might eat dinner with them. He said he was hungry, and the hotel fare did not tempt him. And when Judge Rawdon returned he welcomed him in the same generous spirit, and the evening passed delightfully away. At its close, however, as Mostyn stood gloved and hatted, and the carriage waited for him, he said a few words to Judge Rawdon which changed the mental and social atmosphere. "I wish to have a little talk with you, sir, on a business matter of some importance. At what hour can I see you to-morrow?"

"I am engaged all day until three in the afternoon, Fred. Suppose I call on you about four or half-past?"

"Very well, sir."

But both Ethel and Ruth wondered if it was "very well." A shadow, fleeting as thought, had passed over Judge Rawdon's face when he heard the request for a business interview, and after the young man's departure he lost himself in a reverie which was evidently not a happy one. But he said nothing to the girls, and they were not accustomed to question him.

The next morning, instead of going direct to his office, he stopped at Madam, his mother's house in Gramercy Park. A visit at such an early hour was unusual, and the old lady looked at him in alarm.

"We are well, mother," he said as she rose. "I called to talk to you about a little business." Whereupon Madam sat down, and became suddenly about twenty years younger, for "business" was a word like a watch-cry; she called all her senses together when it was uttered in her presence.

"Business!" she ejaculated sharply. "Whose business?"

"I think I may say the business of the whole family."

"Nay, I am not in it. My business is just as I want it, and I am not going to talk about it—one way or the other."

"Is not Rawdon Court of some interest to you? It has been the home and seat of the family for many centuries. A good many. Mostyn women have been its mistress."

"I never heard of any Mostyn woman who would not have been far happier away from Rawdon Court. It was a Calvary to them all. There was little Nannie Mostyn, who died with her first baby because Squire Anthony struck her in a drunken passion; and the proud Alethia Mostyn, who suffered twenty years' martyrdom from Squire John; and Sara, who took thirty thousand pounds to Squire Hubert, to fling away at the green table; and Harriet, who was made by her husband, Squire Humphrey, to jump a fence when out hunting with him, and was brought home crippled and scarred for life—a lovely girl of twenty who went through agonies for eleven years without aught of love and help, and died alone while he was following a fox; and there was pretty Barbara Mostyn—"

"Come, come, mother. I did not call here this morning to hear the Rawdons abused, and you forget your own marriage. It was a happy one, I am sure. One Rawdon, at least, must be excepted; and I think I treated my wife as a good husband ought to treat a wife."

"Not you! You treated Mary very badly."

"Mother, not even from you—"

"I'll say it again. The little girl was dying for a year or more, and you were so busy making money you never saw it. If she said or looked a little complaint, you moved restless-like and told her 'she moped too much.' As the end came I spoke to you, and you pooh-poohed all I said. She went suddenly, I know, to most people, but she knew it was her last day, and she longed so to see you, that I sent a servant to hurry you home, but she died before you could make up your mind to leave your 'cases.' She and I were alone when she whispered her last message for you—a loving one, too."

"Mother! Mother! Why recall that bitter day? I did not think—I swear I did not think—"

"Never mind swearing. I was just reminding you that the Rawdons have not been the finest specimens of good husbands. They make landlords, and judges, and soldiers, and even loom-lords of a very respectable sort; but husbands! Lord help their poor wives! So you see, as a Mostyn woman, I have no special interest in Rawdon Court."

"You would not like it to go out of the family?"

"I should not worry myself if it did."

"I suppose you know Fred Mostyn has a mortgage on it that the present Squire is unable to lift."

"Aye, Fred told me he had eighty thousand pounds on the old place. I told him he was a fool to put his money on it."

"One of the finest manors and manor-houses in England, mother."

"I have seen it. I was born and brought up near enough to it, I think."

"Eighty thousand pounds is a bagatelle for the place; yet if Fred forces a sale, it may go for that, or even less. I can't bear to think of it."

"Why not buy it yourself?"

"I would lift the mortgage to-morrow if I had the means. I have not at present."

"Well, I am in the same box. You have just spoken as if the Mostyns and Rawdons had an equal interest in Rawdon Court. Very well, then, it cannot be far wrong for Fred Mostyn to have it. Many a Mostyn has gone there as wife and slave. I would dearly like to see one Mostyn go as master."

"I shall get no help from you, then, I understand that."

"I'm Mostyn by birth, I'm only Rawdon by, marriage. The birth-band ties me fast to my family."

"Good morning, mother. You have failed me for the first time in your life."

"If the money had been for you, Edward, or yours—"

"It is—good-by."

She called him back peremptorily, and he returned and stood at the open door.

"Why don't you ask Ethel?"

"I did not think I had the right, mother."

"More right to ask her than I. See what she says. She's Rawdon, every inch of her."

"Perhaps I may. Of course, I can sell securities, but it would be at a sacrifice a great sacrifice at present."

"Ethel has the cash; and, as I said, she is Rawdon—I'm not."

"I wish my father were alive."

"He wouldn't move me—you needn't think that. What I have said to you I would have said to him. Speak to Ethel. I'll be bound she'll listen if Rawdon calls her."

"I don't like to speak to Ethel."

"It isn't what you like to do, it's what you find you'll have to do, that carries the day; and a good thing, too, considering."

"Good morning, again. You are not quite yourself, I think."

"Well, I didn't sleep last night, so there's no wonder if I'm a bit cross this morning. But if I lose my temper, I keep my understanding."

She was really cross by this time. Her son had put her in a position she did not like to assume. No love for Rawdon Court was in her heart. She would rather have advanced the money to buy an American estate. She had been little pleased at Fred's mortgage on the old place, but to the American Rawdons she felt it would prove a white elephant; and the appeal to Ethel was advised because she thought it would amount to nothing. In the first place, the Judge had the strictest idea of the sacredness of the charge committed to

Amelia E. Barr

him as guardian of his daughter's fortune. In the second, Ethel inherited from her Yorkshire ancestry an intense sense of the value and obligations of money. She was an ardent American, and not likely to spend it on an old English manor; and, furthermore, Madam's penetration had discovered a growing dislike in her granddaughter for Fred Mostyn.

"She'd never abide him for a lifelong neighbor," the old lady decided. "It is the Rawdon pride in her. The Rawdon men have condescended to go to Mostyn for wives many and many a time, but never once have the Mostyn men married a Rawdon girl—proud, set-up women, as far as I remember; and Ethel has a way with her just like them. Fred is good enough and nice enough for any girl, and I wonder what is the matter with him! It is a week and more since he was here, and then he wasn't a bit like himself."

At this moment the bell rang and she heard Fred's voice inquiring "if Madam was at home." Instantly she divined the motive of his call. The young man had come to the conclusion the Judge would try to influence his mother, and before meeting him in the afternoon he wished to have some idea of the trend matters were likely to take. His policy—cunning, Madam called it—did not please her. She immediately assured herself that "she wouldn't go against her own flesh and blood for anyone," and his wan face and general air of wretchedness further antagonized her. She asked him fretfully "what he had been doing to himself, for," she added, "it's mainly what we do to ourselves that makes us sick. Was it that everlasting wedding of the Denning girl?"

He flushed angrily, but answered with much of the same desire to annoy, "I suppose it was. I felt it very much. Dora was the loveliest girl in the city. There are none left like her."

"It will be a good thing for New York if that is the case. I'm not one that wants the city to myself, but I can spare Dora STANHOPE, and feel the better for it."

"The most beautiful of God's creatures!"

"You've surely lost your sight or your judgment, Fred. She is just a dusky-skinned girl, with big, brown eyes. You can pick her sort up by the thousand in any large city. And a wandering-hearted, giddy creature, too, that will spread as she goes, no doubt. I'm sorry for Basil Stanhope, he didn't deserve such a fate."

"Indeed, he did not! It is beyond measure too good for him."

"I've always heard that affliction is the surest way to heaven. Dora will lead him that road, and it will be more sure than pleasant. Poor fellow! He'll soon be as ready to curse his wedding-day as Job was to curse his birthday. A costly wife she will be to keep, and misery in the keeping of her. But if you came to talk to me about Dora STANHOPE, I'll cease talking, for I don't find it any great entertainment."

"I came to talk to you about Squire Rawdon."

"What about the Squire? Keep it in your mind that he and I were sweethearts when we were children. I haven't forgotten that fact."

"You know Rawdon Court is mortgaged to me?"

"I've heard you say so—more than once."

"I intend to foreclose the mortgage in September. I find that I can get twice yes, three times—the interest for my money in American securities."

Amelia E. Barr

"How do you know they are securities?"

"Bryce Denning has put me up to several good things."

"Well, if you think good things can come that road, you are a bigger fool than I ever thought you."

"Fool! Madam, I allow no one to call me a fool, especially without reason."

"Reason, indeed! What reason was there in your dillydallying after Dora Denning when she was engaged, and then making yourself like a ghost for her after she is married? As for the good things Bryce Denning offers you in exchange for a grand English manor, take them, and then if I called you not fool before, I will call you fool in your teeth twice over, and much too good for you! Aye, I could call you a worse name when I think of the old Squire—he's two years older than I am—being turned out of his lifelong home. Where is he to go to?"

"If I buy the place, for of course it will have to be sold, he is welcome to remain at Rawdon Court."

"And he would deserve to do it if he were that low-minded; but if I know Squire Percival, he will go to the poor-house first. Fred, you would surely scorn such a dirty thing as selling the old man out of house and home?"

"I want my money, or else I want Rawdon Manor."

"And I have no objections either to your wanting it or having it, but, for goodness' sake, wait until death gives you a decent warrant for buying it."

"I am afraid to delay. The Squire has been very cool with me lately, and my agent tells me the Tyrrel-Rawdons have been visiting him, also that he has asked a great many questions about the Judge and Ethel. He is evidently trying to prevent me getting possession, and I know that old Nicholas Rawdon would give his eyelids to own Rawdon Court. As to the Judge—"

"My son wants none of it. You can make your mind easy on that score."

"I think I behaved very decently, though, of course, no one gives me credit for it; for as soon as I saw I must foreclose in order to get my own I thought at once of Ethel. It seemed to me that if we could love each other the money claims of Mostyn and the inherited claims of Rawdon would both be satisfied. Unfortunately, I found that I could not love Ethel as a wife should be loved."

"And I can tell you, Fred, that Ethel never could have loved you as a husband should be loved. She was a good deal disappointed in you from the very first."

"I thought I made a favorable impression on her."

"In a way. She said you played the piano nicely; but Ethel is all for handsome men, tall, erect six-footers, with a little swing and swagger to them. She thought you small and finicky. But Ethel's rich enough to have her fancy, I hope."

"It is little matter now what she thought. I can't please every one."

"No, it's rather harder to do that than most people think it is. I would please my conscience first of all, Fred. That's the point worth mentioning. And I shall just remind you of one thing more: your money all in a lump on Rawdon Manor is safe. It is in one place, and in such shape as it can't run away nor be smuggled away by any man's trickery. Now, then, turn your eighty thousand pounds into dollars, and divide them among a score of securities, and you'll soon find out that a fortune may be easily squandered when it is in a great many hands, and that what looks satisfactory enough when reckoned up on paper doesn't often realize in hard money to the same tune. I've said all now I am going to say."

"Thank you for the advice given me. I will take it as far as I can. This afternoon the Judge has promised to talk over the business with me."

"The Judge never saw Rawdon Court, and he cares nothing about it, but he can give you counsel about the 'good things' Bryce Denning offers you. And you may safely listen to it, for, right or wrong, I see plainly it is your own advice you will take in the long run."

Mostyn laughed pleasantly and went back to his hotel to think over the facts gleaned from his conversation with Madam. In the first place, he understood that any overt act against Squire Rawdon would be deeply resented by his American relatives. But then he reminded himself that his own relationship with them was merely sentiment. He had now nothing to hope for in the way of money. Madam's apparently spontaneous and truthful assertion, that the Judge cared nothing for Rawdon Court, was, however, very satisfactory to him. He had been foolish enough to think that the thing he desired so passionately was of equal value in the estimation of others. He saw now that he was wrong, and he then remembered that he had never found Judge Rawdon to evince either interest or curiosity about the family home.

If he had been a keen observer, the Judge's face when he called might have given his comfortable feelings some pause. It was contracted, subtle, intricate, but he came forward with a congratulation on Mostyn's improved appearance. "A few weeks at the seaside would do you good," he added, and Mostyn answered, "I think of going to Newport for a month."

"And then?"

"I want your opinion about that. McLean advises me to see the country—to go to Chicago, St. Louis, Denver, cross the Rockies, and on to California. It seems as if that would be a grand summer programme. But my lawyer writes me that the man in charge at Mostyn is cutting too much timber and is generally too extravagant. Then there is the question of Rawdon Court. My finances will not let me carry the mortgage on it longer, unless I buy the place."

"Are you thinking of that as probable?"

"Yes. It will have to be sold. And Mostyn seems to be the natural owner after Rawdon. The Mostyns have married Rawdons so frequently that we are almost like one family, and Rawdon Court lies, as it were, at Mostyn's gate. The Squire is now old, and too easily persuaded for his own welfare, and I hear the Tyrrel-Rawdons have been visiting him. Such a thing would have been incredible a few years ago."

"Who are the Tyrrel-Rawdons? I have no acquaintance with them."

"They are the descendants of that Tyrrel-Rawdon who a century ago married a handsome girl who was only an innkeeper's daughter. He was of course disowned and disinherited, and his children sank to the lowest social grade. Then when power-loom weaving was introduced they went to

Amelia E. Barr

the mills, and one of them was clever and saved money and built a little mill of his own, and his son built a much larger one, and made a great deal of money, and became Mayor of Leeds. The next generation saw the Tyrrel-Rawdons the largest loom-lords in Yorkshire. One of the youngest generation was my opponent in the last election and beat me—a Radical fellow beats the Conservative candidate always where weavers and spinners hold the vote but I thought it my duty to uphold the Mostyn banner. You know the Mostyns have always been Tories and Conservatives."

"Excuse me, but I am afraid I am ignorant concerning Mostyn politics. I take little interest in the English parties."

"Naturally. Well, I hope you will take an interest in my affairs and give me your advice about the sale of Rawdon Court."

"I think my advice would be useless. In the first place, I never saw the Court. My father had an old picture of it, which has somehow disappeared since his death, but I cannot say that even this picture interested me at all. You know I am an American, born on the soil, and very proud of it. Then, as you are acquainted with all the ins and outs of the difficulties and embarrassments, and I know nothing at all about them, you would hardly be foolish enough to take my opinion against your own. I suppose the Squire is in favor of your buying the Court?"

"I never named the subject to him. I thought perhaps he might have written to you on the matter. You are the last male of the house in that line."

"He has never written to me about the Court. Then, I am not the last male. From what you say, I think the Tyrrel-Rawdons could easily supply an heir to Rawdon."

"That is the thing to be avoided. It would be a great offense to the county families."

"Why should they be considered? A Rawdon is always a Rawdon."

"But a cotton spinner, sir! A mere mill-owner!"

"Well, I do not feel with you and the other county people in that respect. I think a cotton spinner, giving bread to a thousand families, is a vastly more respectable and important man than a fox-hunting, idle landlord. A mill-owning Rawdon might do a deal of good in the sleepy old village of Monk-Rawdon."

"Your sentiments are American, not English, sir."

"As I told you, we look at things from very different standpoints."

"Do you feel inclined to lift the mortgage yourself, Judge?"

"I have not the power, even if I had the inclination to do so. My money is well invested, and I could not, at this time, turn bonds and securities into cash without making a sacrifice not to be contemplated. I confess, however, that if the Court has to be sold, I should like the Tyrrel-Rawdons to buy it. I dare say the picture of the offending youth is still in the gallery, and I have heard my mother say that what is another's always yearns for its lord. Driven from his heritage for Love's sake, it would be at least interesting if Gold gave back to his children what Love lost them."

"That is pure sentiment. Surely it would be more natural that the Mostyns should succeed the Rawdons. We have, as it were, bought the right with at least a dozen intermarriages."

"That also is pure sentiment. Gold at last will carry the succession."

"But not your gold, I infer?"

"Not my gold; certainly not."

"Thank you for your decisive words They make my course clear."

"That is well. As to your summer movements, I am equally unable to give you advice. I think you need the sea for a month, and after that McLean's scheme is good. And a return to Mostyn to look after your affairs is equally good. If I were you, I should follow my inclinations. If you put your heart into anything, it is well done and enjoyed; if you do a thing because you think you ought to do it, failure and disappointment are often the results. So do as you want to do; it is the only advice I can offer you."

"Thank you, sir. It is very acceptable. I may leave for Newport to-morrow. I shall call on the ladies in the morning."

"I will tell them, but it is just possible that they, too, go to the country to-morrow, to look after a little cottage on the Hudson we occupy in the summer. Good-by, and I hope you will soon recover your usual health."

Then the Judge lifted his hat, and with a courteous movement left the room. His face had the same suave urbanity of expression, but he could hardly restrain the passion in his heart. Placid as he looked when he entered his house, he threw off all pretenses as soon as he reached his room. The Yorkshire spirit which Ethel had declared found him out once in three hundred and sixty-four days and twenty-three hours was then in full possession. The American Judge had disappeared. He looked as like his ancestors as anything outside of a painted picture could do. His flushed face, his flashing eyes, his passionate exclamations, the stamp of his foot, the blow of his hand, the threatening attitude of his whole figure was but a replica of his great-grandfather, Anthony Rawdon, giving Radicals at the hustings or careless keepers at the kennels "a bit of his mind."

"'Mostyn, seems to be the natural owner of Rawdon! Rawdon Court lies at Mostyn's gate! Natural that the Mostyns should succeed the Rawdons! Bought the right by a dozen intermarriages!' Confound the impudent rascal! Does he think I will see Squire Rawdon rogued out of his home? Not if I can help it! Not if Ethel can help it! Not if heaven and earth can help it! He's a downright rascal! A cool, unruffled, impudent rascal!" And these ejaculations were followed by a bitter, biting, blasting hailstorm of such epithets as could only be written with one letter and a dash.

But the passion of imprecation cooled and satisfied his anger in this its first impetuous outbreak, and he sat down, clasped the arms of his chair, and gave himself a peremptory order of control. In a short time he rose, bathed his head and face in cold water, and began to dress for dinner. And as he stood before the glass he smiled at the restored color and calm of his countenance.

"You are a prudent lawyer," he said sarcastically. "How many actionable words have you just uttered! If the devil and Fred Mostyn have been listening, they can, as mother says, 'get the law on you'; but I think Ethel and I and the law will be a match even for the devil and Fred Mostyn." Then, as he slowly went downstairs, he repeated to himself, "Mostyn seems to be the natural owner of Rawdon. No, sir, neither natural nor legal owner. Rawdon Court lies at Mostyn gate. Not yet. Mostyn lies at Rawdon gate. Natural that the

Mostyns should succeed the Rawdons. Power of God!
Neither in this generation nor the next."

And at the same moment Mostyn, having thought over his
interview with Judge Rawdon, walked thoughtfully to a
window and muttered to himself: "Whatever was the matter
with the old man? Polite as a courtier, but something was
wrong. The room felt as if there was an iceberg in it, and he
kept his right hand in his pocket. I believe he was afraid I
would shake hands with him—it is Ethel, I suppose.
Naturally he is disappointed. Wanted her at Rawdon. Well, it
is a pity, but I really cannot! Oh, Dora! Dora! My heart, my
hungry and thirsty heart calls you! Burning with love, dying
with longing, I am waiting for you!"

The dinner passed pleasantly enough, but both Ethel and
Ruth noticed the Judge was under strong but well-controlled
feeling. While servants were present it passed for high
spirits, but as soon as the three were alone in the library, the
excitement took at once a serious aspect.

"My dears," he said, standing up and facing them, "I have
had a very painful interview with Fred Mostyn. He holds a
mortgage over Rawdon Court, and is going to press it in
September—that is, he proposes to sell the place in order to
obtain his money—and the poor Squire!" He ceased
speaking, walked across the room and back again, and
appeared greatly disturbed.

"What of the Squire?" asked Ruth.

"God knows, Ruth. He has no other home."

"Why is this thing to be done? Is there no way to prevent it?"

"Mostyn wants the money, he says, to invest in American

securities. He does not. He wants to force a sale, so that he may buy the place for the mortgage, and then either keep it for his pride, or more likely resell it to the Tyrrel-Rawdons for double the money." Then with gradually increasing passion he repeated in a low, intense voice the remarks which Mostyn had made, and which had so infuriated the Judge. Before he had finished speaking the two women had caught his temper and spirit. Ethel's face was white with anger, her eyes flashing, her whole attitude full of fight. Ruth was troubled and sorrowful, and she looked anxiously at the Judge for some solution of the condition. It was Ethel who voiced the anxiety. "Father," she asked, "what is to be done? What can you do?"

"Nothing, I am sorry to say, Ethel. My money is absolutely tied up—for this year, at any rate. I cannot touch it without wronging others as well as myself, nor yet without the most ruinous sacrifice."

"If I could do anything, I would not care at what sacrifice."

"You can do all that is necessary, Ethel, and you are the only person who can. You have at least eight hundred thousand dollars in cash and negotiable securities. Your mother's fortune is all yours, with its legitimate accruements, and it was left at your own disposal after your twenty-first birthday. It has been at your own disposal WITH MY CONSENT since your nineteenth birthday."

"Then, father, we need not trouble about the Squire. I wish with all my heart to make his home sure to him as long as he lives. You are a lawyer, you know what ought to be done."

"Good girl! I knew what you would say and do, or I should not have told you the trouble there was at Rawdon. Now, I propose we all make a visit to Rawdon Court, see the Squire and the property, and while there perfect such arrangements as seem kindest and wisest. Ruth, how soon can we be ready to sail?"

"Father, do you really mean that we are to go to England?"

"It is the only thing to do. I must see that all is as Mostyn says. I must not let you throw your money away."

"That is only prudent," said Ruth, "and we can be ready for the first steamer if you wish it."

"I am delighted, father. I long to see England; more than all, I long to see Rawdon. I did not know until this moment how much I loved it."

"Well, then, I will have all ready for us to sail next Saturday. Say nothing about it to Mostyn. He will call to-morrow morning to bid you good-by before leaving for Newport with McLean. Try and be out."

"I shall certainly be out," said Ethel. "I do not wish ever to see his face again, and I must see grandmother and tell her what we are going to do."

"I dare say she guesses already. She advised me to ask you about the mortgage. She knew what you would say."

"Father, who are the Tyrrel-Rawdons?"

Then the Judge told the story of the young Tyrrel-Rawdon, who a century ago had lost his world for Love, and Ethel said "she liked him better than any Rawdon she had ever heard of."

"Except your father, Ethel."

"Except my father; my dear, good father. And I am glad that Love did not always make them poor. They must now be rich, if they want to buy the Court."

"They are rich manufacturers. Mostyn is much annoyed that the Squire has begun to notice them. He says one of the grandsons of the Tyrrel-Rawdons, disinherited for love's sake, came to America some time in the forties. I asked your grandmother if this story was true. She said it is quite true; that my father was his friend in the matter, and that it was his reports about America which made them decide to try their fortune in New York."

"Does she know what became of him?"

"No. In his last letter to them he said he had just joined a party going to the gold fields of California. That was in 1850. He never wrote again. It is likely he perished on the terrible journey across the plains. Many thousands did."

"When I am in England I intend to call upon these Tyrrel-Rawdons. I think I shall like them. My heart goes out to them. I am proud of this bit of romance in the family."

"Oh, there is plenty of romance behind you, Ethel. When you see the old Squire standing at the entrance to the Manor House, you may see the hags of Cressy and Agincourt, of Marston and Worcester behind him. And the Rawdon women have frequently been daughters of Destiny. Many of them have lived romances that would be incredible if written down. Oh, Ethel, dear, we cannot, we cannot for our lives, let the old home fall into the hands of strangers. At any rate, if on inspection we think it wrong to interfere, I can at least try and get the children of the disinherited Tyrrel back to their home. Shall we leave it at this point for the present?"

This decision was agreeable to all, and then the few preparations necessary for the journey were talked over, and in this happy discussion the evening passed rapidly. The dream of Ethel's life had been this visit to the home of her family, and to go as its savior was a consummation of the pleasure that filled her with loving pride. She could not sleep for her waking dreams. She made all sorts of resolutions about the despised Tyrrel-Rawdons. She intended to show the proud, indolent world of the English land-aristocracy that Americans, just as well born as themselves, respected business energy and enterprise; and she had other plans and propositions just as interesting and as full of youth's impossible enthusiasm.

In the morning she went to talk the subject over with her grandmother. The old lady received the news with affected indifference. She said, "It mattered nothing to her who sat in Rawdon's seat; but she would not hear Mostyn blamed for seeking his right. Money and sentiment are no kin," she added, "and Fred has no sentiment about Rawdon. Why should he? Only last summer Rawdon kept him out of Parliament, and made him spend a lot of money beside. He's right to get even with the family if he can."

"But the old Squire! He is now—"

"I know; he's older than I am. But Squire Percival has had his day, and Fred would not do anything out of the way to him—he could not; the county would make both Mostyn and Rawdon very uncomfortable places to live in, if he did."

"If you turn a man out of his home when he is eighty years old, I think that is 'out of the way.' And Mr. Mostyn is not to be trusted. I wouldn't trust him as far as I could see him."

"Highty-tighty! He has not asked you to trust him. You lost

your chance there, miss."

"Grandmother, I am astonished at you!"

"Well, it was a mean thing to say, Ethel; but I like Fred, and I see the rest of my family are against him. It's natural for Yorkshire to help the weakest side. But there, Fred can do his own fighting, I'll warrant. He's not an ordinary man."

"I'm sorry to say he isn't, grandmother. If he were he would speak without a drawl, and get rid of his monocle, and not pay such minute attention to his coats and vests and walking sticks."

Then Ethel proceeded to explain her resolves with regard to the Tyrrel-Rawdons. "I shall pay them the greatest attention," she said. "It was a noble thing in young Tyrrel-Rawdon to give up everything for honorable love, and I think everyone ought to have stood by him."

"That wouldn't have done at all. If Tyrrel had been petted as you think he ought to have been, every respectable young man and woman in the county would have married where their fancy led them; and the fancies of young people mostly lead them to the road it is ruin to take."

"From what Fred Mostyn says, Tyrrel's descendants seem to have taken a very respectable road."

"I've nothing to say for or against them. It's years and years since I laid eyes on any of the family. Your grandfather helped one of the young men to come to America, and I remember his mother getting into a passion about it. She was a fat woman in a Paisley shawl and a love-bird on her bonnet. I saw his sister often. She weighed about twelve stone, and had red hair and red cheeks and bare red elbows.

She was called a 'strapping lass.' That is quite a complimentary term in the West Riding."

"Please, grandmother, I don't want to hear any more. In two weeks I shall be able to judge for myself. Since then there have been two generations, and if a member of the present one is fit for Parliament—"

"That's nothing. We needn't look for anything specially refined in Parliament in these days. There's another thing. These Tyrrel-Rawdons are chapel people. The rector of Rawdon church would not marry Tyrrel to his low-born love, and so they went to the Methodist preacher, and after that to the Methodist chapel. That put them down, more than you can imagine here in America."

"It was a shame! Methodists are most respectable people."

"I'm saying nothing contrary."

"The President is a Methodist."

"I never asked what he was. I am a Church of England woman, you know that. Born and bred in the Church, baptized, confirmed, and married in the Church, and I was always taught it was the only proper Church for gentlemen and gentlewomen to be saved in. However, English Methodists often go back to the Church when they get rich."

"Church or chapel makes no difference to me, grandmother. If people are only good."

"To be sure; but you won't be long in England until you'll find out that some things make a great deal of difference. Do you know your father was here this morning? He wanted me to go with you—a likely, thing."

"But, grandmother, do come. We will take such good care of you, and—"

"I know, but I'd rather keep my old memories of Yorkshire than get new-fashioned ones. All is changed. I can tell that by what Fred says. My three great friends are dead. They have left children and grandchildren, of course, but I don't want to make new acquaintances at my age, unless I have the picking of them. No, I shall get Miss Hillis to go with me to my little cabin on the Jersey coast. We'll take our knitting and the fresh novels, and I'll warrant we'll see as much of the new men and women in them as will more than satisfy us. But you must write me long letters, and tell me everything about the Squire and the way he keeps house, and I don't care if you fill up the paper with the Tyrrel-Rawdons."

"I will write you often, Granny, and tell you everything."

"I shouldn't wonder if you come across Dora Stanhope, but I wouldn't ask her to Rawdon. She'll mix some cup of bother if you do."

"I know."

In such loving and intimate conversation the hours sped quickly, and Ethel could not bear to cut short her visit. It was nearly five when she left Gramercy Park, but the day being lovely, and the avenue full of carriages and pedestrians, she took the drive at its enforced tardiness without disapproval. Almost on entering the avenue from Madison Square there was a crush, and her carriage came to a standstill. She was then opposite the store of a famous English saddler, and near her was an open carriage occupied by a middle-aged gentleman in military uniform. He appeared to be waiting for someone, and in a moment or two a young man came out of the saddlery store, and with a pleasant laugh entered the

Amelia E. Barr

carriage. It was the Apollo of her dreams, the singer of the Holland House pavement. She could not doubt it. His face, his figure, his walk, and the pleasant smile with which he spoke to his companion were all positive characteristics. She had forgotten none of them. His dress was altered to suit the season, but that was an improvement; for divested of his heavy coat, and clothed only in a stylish afternoon suit, his tall, fine figure showed to great advantage; and Ethel told herself that he was even handsomer than she had supposed him to be.

Almost as soon as he entered his carriage there was a movement, and she hoped her driver might advance sufficiently to make recognition possible, but some feeling, she knew not what, prevented her giving any order leading to this result. Perhaps she had an instinctive presentiment that it was best to leave all to Destiny. Toward the upper part of the avenue the carriage of her eager observation came to a stand before a warehouse of antique furniture and bric-a-brac, and, as it did so, a beautiful woman ran down the steps, and Apollo, for so Ethel had mentally called him, went hurriedly to meet her. Finally her coachman passed the party, and there was a momentary recognition. He was bending forward, listening to something the lady was saying, when the vehicles almost touched each other. He flashed a glance at them, and met the flash of Ethel's eyes full of interest and curiosity.

It was over in a moment, but in that moment Ethel saw his astonishment and delight, and felt her own eager questioning answered. Then she was joyous and full of hope, for "these two silent meetings are promises," she said to Ruth. "I feel sure I shall see him again, and then we shall speak to each other."

"I hope you are not allowing yourself to feel too much

interest in this man, Ethel; he is very likely married."

"Oh, no! I am sure he is not, Ruth."

"How can you be sure? You know nothing about him."

"I cannot tell HOW I know, nor WHY I know, but I believe what I feel; and he is as much interested in me as I am in him. I confess that is a great deal."

"You may never see him again."

"I shall expect to see him next winter, he evidently lives in New York."

"The lady you saw may be his wife. Don't be interested in any man on unknown ground, Ethel. It is not prudent—it is not right."

"Time will show. He will very likely be looking for me this summer at Newport and elsewhere. He will be glad to see me when I come home. Don't worry, Ruth. It is all right."

"Fred called soon after you went out this morning. He left for Newport this afternoon. He will be at sea now."

"And we shall be there in a few days. When I am at the seaside I always feel a delicious torpor; yet Nelly Baldwin told me she loved an Atlantic passage because she had such fun on board. You have crossed several times, Ruth; is it fun or torpor?"

"All mirth at sea soon fades away, Ethel. Passengers are a very dull class of people, and they know it; they rebel against it, but every hour it becomes more natural to be dull. Very soon all mentally accommodate themselves to being bored, dreamy and dreary. Then, as soon as it is dark, comes that old mysterious, hungering sound of the sea; and I for one listen till I can bear it no longer, and so steal away to bed with a pain in my heart."

"I think I shall like the ocean. There are games, and books, and company, and dinners, and other things."

"Certainly, and you can think yourself happy, until gradually a contented cretinism steals over you, body and mind."

"No, no!" said Ethel enthusiastically. "I shall do according to Swinburne—

"'Have therefore in my heart, and in my mouth,
The sound of song that mingles North and South;
And in my Soul the sense of all the Sea!'"

And Ruth laughed at her dramatic attitude, and answered: "The soul of all the sea is a contented cretinism, Ethel. But in ten days we may be in Yorkshire. And then, my dear, you may meet your Prince—some fine Yorkshire gentleman."

"I have strictly and positively promised myself that my Prince shall be a fine American gentleman."

"My dear Ethel, it is very seldom

"'the time, and the place,
And the Loved One, come together.'"

"I live in the land of good hope, Ruth, and my hopes will be realized."

"We shall see."

PART THIRD

"I WENT DOWN INTO THE GARDEN TO SEE IF THE POMEGRANATES BUDDED.

Song of Solomon, VI. 11.

CHAPTER VII

IT was a lovely afternoon on the last day of May. The sea and all the toil and travail belonging to it was overpass, and Judge Rawdon, Ruth and Ethel were driving in lazy, blissful contentment through one of the lovely roads of the West Riding. On either hand the beautifully cut hedges were white and sweet, and a caress of scent—the soul of the hawthorne flower enfolded them. Robins were singing on the topmost sprays, and the linnet's sweet babbling was heard from the happy nests in its secret places; while from some unseen steeple the joyful sound of chiming bells made music between heaven and earth fit for bands of traveling angels.

They had dined at a wayside inn on jugged hare, roast beef, and Yorkshire pudding, clotted cream and haver (oaten) bread, and the careless stillness of physical well-being and of minds at ease needed no speech, but the mutual smiling nod of intimate sympathy. For the sense of joy and beauty which makes us eloquent is far inferior to that sense which makes us silent.

This exquisite pause in life was suddenly ended by an exclamation from the Judge. They were at the great iron gates of Rawdon Park, and soon were slowly traversing its woody solitudes. The soft light, the unspeakable green of the turf, the voice of ancient days murmuring in the great oak trees, the deer asleep among the ferns, the stillness of the summer afternoon filling the air with drowsy peace this was the atmosphere into which they entered. Their road through this grand park of three hundred acres was a wide, straight avenue shaded with beech trees. The green turf on either hand was starred with primroses. In the deep undergrowth, ferns waved and fanned each other, and the scent of hidden violets saluted as they passed. Drowsily, as if half asleep, the blackbirds whistled their couplets, and in the thickest hedges the little brown thrushes sang softly to their brooding mates. For half an hour they kept this heavenly path, and then a sudden turn brought them their first sight of the old home.

It was a stately, irregular building of red brick, sandaled and veiled in ivy. The numerous windows were all latticed, the chimneys in picturesque stacks, the sloping roof made of flags of sandstone. It stood in the center of a large garden, at the bottom of which ran a babbling little river—a cheerful tongue of life in the sweet, silent place. They crossed it by a pretty bridge, and in a few minutes stood at the great door of the mansion. It was wide open, and the Squire, with outstretched hands, rose to meet them. While yet upon the threshold he kissed both Ethel and Ruth, and, clasping the Judge's hand, gazed at him with such a piercing, kindly look that the eyes of both men filled with tears.

He led them into the hall, and standing there he seemed almost a part of it. In his youth he had been a son of Anak, and his great size had been matched by his great strength. His stature was still large, his face broad and massive, and an abundance of snow-white hair emphasized the dignity of a countenance which age had made nobler. The generations of eight hundred years were crystallized in this benignant old man, looking with such eager interest into the faces of his strange kindred from a far-off land.

In the evening they sat together in the old hall talking of the Rawdons. "There is great family of us, living and dead," said the Squire, "and I count them all my friends. Bare is the back that has no kin behind it. That is not our case. Eight hundred years ago there was a Rawdon in Rawdon, and one has never been wanting since. Saxon, Danish, Norman, and Stuart kings have been and gone their way, and we remain; and I can tell you every Rawdon born since the House of Hanover came to England. We have had our share in all England's strife and glory, for if there was ever a fight going on anywhere Rawdon was never far off. Yes, we can string the centuries together in the battle flags we have won. See there!" he cried, pointing to two standards interwoven above the central chimney-piece; "one was taken from the Paynim in the first Crusade, and the other my grandson took in Africa. It seems but yesterday, and Queen Victoria gave him the Cross for it. Poor lad, he had it on when he died. It went to the grave with him. I wouldn't have it touched. I fancy the Rawdons would know it. No one dare say they don't. I think they meddle a good deal more with this life than we count on."

The days that followed were days in The House Wonderful. It held the treasure-trove of centuries; all its rooms were full of secrets. Even the common sitting-room had an antique homeliness that provoked questions as to the dates of its furniture and the whereabouts of its wall cupboards and hidden recesses. Its china had the marks of forgotten makers, its silver was puzzling with half-obliterated names and dates, its sideboard of oak was black with age and full of table accessories, the very names of which were forgotten. For this house had not been built in the ordinary sense, it had grown through centuries; grown out of desire and necessity, just as a tree grows, and was therefore fit and beautiful. And it was no wonder that about every room floated the perfume of ancient things and the peculiar family aura that had saturated all the inanimate objects around them.

In a few days, life settled itself to orderly occupations. The Squire was a late riser; the Judge and his family breakfasted very early. Then the two women had a ride in the park, or wandered in the garden, or sat reading, or sewing, or writing in some of the sweet, fair rooms. Many visitors soon appeared, and there were calls to return and courtesies to accept. Among these visitors the Tyrrel-Rawdons were the earliest. The representatives of that family were Nicholas Rawdon and his wife Lydia. Nicholas Rawdon was a large, stout man, very arrogant, very complete, very alert for this world, and not caring much about the other. He was not pleased at Judge Rawdon's visit, but thought it best to be cousinly until his cousin interfered with his plans—"rights" he called them—"and then!" and his "THEN" implied a great deal, for Nicholas Rawdon was a man incapable of conceiving the idea of loving an enemy.

His wife was a pleasant, garrulous woman, who interested Ethel very much. Her family was her chief topic of conversation. She had two daughters, one of whom had married a baronet, "a man with money and easy to manage"; and the other, "a rich cotton lord in Manchester."

"They haven't done badly," she said confidentially, "and it's a great thing to get girls off your hands early. Adelaide and Martha were well educated and suitable, but, "she added with a glow of pride, "you should see my John Thomas. He's manager of the mill, and he loves the mill, and he knows every pound of warp or weft that comes in or goes out of the mill; and what his father would do without him, I'm sure I don't know. And he is a member of Parliament, too—Radical ticket. Won over Mostyn. Wiped Mostyn out pretty well. That was a thing to do, wasn't it?"

"I suppose Mr. Mostyn was the Conservative candidate?"

"You may be sure of that. But my John Thomas doesn't blame him for it—the gentry have to be Conservatives. John Thomas said little against his politics; he just set the crowd laughing at his ways—his dandified ways. And he tried to wear one eyeglass, and let it fall, and fall, and then told the men 'he couldn't manage half a pair of spectacles; but he could manage their interests and fight for their rights,' and such like talk. And he walked like Mostyn, and he talked like Mostyn, and spread out his legs, and twirled his walking stick like Mostyn, and asked them 'if they would wish him to go to Parliament in that kind of a shape, as he'd try and do it if they wanted a tailor-made man'; and they laughed him down, and then he spoke reasonable to them. John Thomas knows what Yorkshire weavers want, and he just promised them everything they had set their hearts on; and so they sent him to Parliament, and Mostyn went to America, where, perhaps, they'll teach him that a man's life is worth a bit more than a bird or a rabbit. Mostyn is all for preserving game, and his father was a mean creature. When one thinks of his father, one has to excuse the young man a little bit."

"I saw a good deal of Mr. Mostyn in New York," said Ethel. "He used to speak highly of his father."

"I'll warrant he did; and he ought to keep at it, for he's the only one in this world that will use his tongue for that end. Old Samuel Mostyn never learned to live godly or even manly, but after his death he ceased to do evil, and that, I've no doubt, often feels like a blessing to them that had to live anyway near to him. But my John Thomas!"

"Oh," cried Ethel, laughing, "you must not tell me so much about John Thomas; he might not like it."

"John Thomas can look all he does and all he says straight in the face. You may talk of him all day, and find nothing to say that a good girl like you might not listen to. I should have brought him with us, but he's away now taking a bit of a holiday. I'm sure he needs it."

"Where is he taking his holiday?"

"Why, he went with a cousin to show him the sights of London; but somehow they got through London sights very quick, and thought they might as well put Paris in. I wish they hadn't. I don't trust foreigners and foreign ways, and they don't have the same kind of money as ours; but Nicholas says I needn't worry; he is sure that our John Thomas, if change is to make, will make it to suit himself."

"How soon will he be home?"

"I might say to-day or any other early day. He's been idling for a month now, and his father says 'the very looms are calling out for him.' I'll bring him to see you just as soon as he comes home, looms or no looms, and he'll be fain to come. No one appreciates a pretty girl more than John Thomas does."

So the days passed sweetly and swiftly onward, and there was no trouble in them. Such business as was to be done went on behind the closed doors of the Squire's office, and with no one present but himself, Judge Rawdon, and the attorneys attached to the Rawdon and Mostyn estates. And as there were no entanglements and no possible reason for disputing, a settlement was quickly arrived at. Then, as Mostyn's return was uncertain, an attorney's messenger, properly accredited, was sent to America to procure his signatures. Allowing for unforeseen delays, the perfected papers of release might certainly be on hand by the fifteenth of July, and it was proposed on the first of August to give a dinner and dance in return for the numerous courtesies the

American Rawdons had received.

As this date approached Ruth and Ethel began to think of a visit to London. They wanted new gowns and many other pretty things, and why not go to London for them? The journey was but a few hours, and two or three days' shopping in Regent Street and Piccadilly would be delightful. "We will make out a list of all we need this afternoon," said Ruth, "and we might as well go to-morrow morning as later," and at this moment a servant entered with the mail. Ethel lifted her letter with an exclamation. "It is from Dora," she said, and her voice had a tone of annoyance in it. "Dora is in London, at the Savoy. She wants to see me very much."

"I am so sorry. We have been so happy."

"I don't think she will interfere much, Ruth."

"My dears," said Judge Rawdon, "I have a letter from Fred Mostyn. He is coming home. He will be in London in a day or two."

"Why is he coming, father?"

"He says he has a proposal to make about the Manor. I wish he were not coming. No one wants his proposal." Then the breakfast-table, which had been so gay, became silent and depressed, and presently the Judge went away without exhibiting further interest in the London journey.

"I do wish Dora would let us alone," said Ruth. "She always brings disappointment or worry of some kind. And I wonder what is the meaning of this unexpected London visit. I thought she was in Holland."

"She said in her last letter that London would be impossible before August."

"Is it an appointment—or a coincidence?"

And Ethel, lifting her shoulders sarcastically, as if in hostile surrender to the inevitable, answered:

"It is a fatality!"

CHAPTER VIII

THREE days afterward Ethel called on Dora Stanhope at the Savoy. She found her alone, and she had evidently been crying. Indeed, she frankly admitted the fact, declaring that she had been "so bored and so homesick, that she relieved she had cried her beauty away." She glanced at Ethel's radiant face and neat fresh toilet with envy, and added, "I am so glad to see you, Ethel. But I was sure that you would come as soon as you knew I wanted you."

"Oh, indeed, Dora, you must not make yourself too sure of such a thing as that! I really came to London to get some new gowns. I have been shopping all morning."

"I thought you had come in answer to my letter. I was expecting you. That is the reason I did not go out with Basil."

"Don't you expect a little too much, Dora? I have a great many interests and duties—"

"I used to be first."

"When a girl marries she is supposed to—"

"Please don't talk nonsense. Basil does not take the place of everyone and everything else. I think we are often very tired of each other. This morning, when I was telling him what trouble I had with my maid, Julia, he actually yawned. He tried to smother the yawn, but he could not, and of course the honeymoon is over when your bridegroom yawns in your face while you are telling him your troubles."

"I should think you would be glad it was over. Of all the words in the English language 'honeymoon' is the most ridiculous and imbecile."

"I suppose when you get married you will take a honeymoon."

"I shall have more sense and more selfishness. A girl could hardly enter a new life through a medium more trying. I am sure it would need long-tested affections and the sweetest of tempers to make it endurable."

"I cannot imagine what you mean."

"I mean that all traveling just after marriage is a great blunder. Traveling makes the sunniest disposition hasty and peevish, for women don't love changes as men do. Not one in a thousand is seen at her best while traveling, and the majority are seen at their very worst. Then there is the discomfort and desolation of European hotels—their mysterious methods and hours, and the ways of foreigners, which are not as our ways."

"Don't talk of them, Ethel. They are dreadful places, and such queer people."

"Add to these troubles ignorance of language and coinage, the utter weariness of railway travel, the plague of customs, the trunk that won't pack, the trains that won't wait, the tiresome sight-seeing, the climatic irritability, broiling suns, headache, loneliness, fretfulness—consequently the pitiful boredom of the new husband."

"Ethel, what you say is certainly too true. I am weary to death of it all. I want to be at Newport with mother, who is having a lovely time there. Of course Basil is very nice to me, and yet there have been little tiffs and struggles—very gentle ones—for the mastery, which he is not going to get. To-day he wanted me to go with him and Canon Shackleton to see something or other about the poor of London. I would not do it. I am so lonely, Ethel, I want to see some one. I feel fit to cry all the time. I like Basil best of anyone in the world, but—"

"But in the solitude of a honeymoon among strangers you find out that the person you like best in the world can bore you as badly as the person you don't like at all. Is that so?"

"Exactly. Just fancy if we were among our friends in Newport. I should have some pleasure in dressing and looking lovely. Why should I dress here? There is no one to see me."

"Basil."

"Of course, but Basil spends all the time in visiting cathedrals and clergymen. If we go out, it is to see something about the poor, or about schools and such like. We were not in London two hours until he was off to Westminster Abbey, and I didn't care a cent about the old place. He says I must not ask him to go to theaters, but historical old houses don't interest me at all. What does it matter if Cromwell slept in a certain ancient shabby room? And as for all the palaces I have seen, my father's house is a great deal handsomer, and more convenient, and more comfortable, and I wish I were there. I hate Europe, and England I hate worst of all."

"You have not seen England. We are all enraptured with its beauty and its old houses and pleasant life."

"You are among friends—at home, as it were. I have heard all about Rawdon Court. Fred Mostyn told me. He is going to buy it."

"When?"

"Some time this fall. Then next year he will entertain us, and that will be a little different to this desolate hotel, I think."

"How long will you be in London?"

"I cannot say. We are invited to Stanhope Castle, but I don't want to go there. We stayed with the Stanhopes a week when we first came over. They were then in their London house, and I got enough of them."

"Did you dislike the family?"

"No, I cared nothing about them. They just bored me. They are extremely religious. We had prayers night and morning, and a prayer before and after every meal. They read only very good books, and the Honorable Misses Stanhope sew for the poor old women and teach the poor young ones. They work harder than anyone I ever knew, and they call it 'improving the time.' They thought me a very silly, reckless young woman, and I think they all prayed for me. One night after they had sung some very nice songs they asked me to play, and I began with 'My Little Brown Rose'—you know they all adore the negro—and little by little I dropped into the funniest coon songs I knew, and oh how they laughed! Even the old lord stroked his knees and laughed out loud, while the young ladies laughed into their handkerchiefs. Lady Stanhope was the only one who comprehended I was guying them; and she looked at me with half-shut eyes in a way that would have spoiled some girls' fun. It only made me the merrier. So I tried to show them a cake walk, but the old lord rose then and said 'I must be tired, and they would excuse me.' Somehow I could not manage him. Basil was at a workman's concert, and when he came home I think there were some advices and remonstrances, but Basil never told me. I felt as if they were all glad when I went away, and I don't wish to go to the Castle—and I won't go either."

"But if Basil wishes to go—"

"He can go alone. I rather think Fred Mostyn will be here in a few days, and he will take me to places that Basil will not—innocent places enough, Ethel, so you need not look so shocked. Why do you not ask me to Rawdon Court?"

"Because I am only a guest there. I have no right to ask you."

"I am sure if you told Squire Rawdon how fond you are of me, and how lonely I am, he would tell you to send for me."

"I do not believe he would. He has old-fashioned ideas about newly married people. He would hardly think it possible that you would be willing to go anywhere without Basil—yet."

"He could ask Basil too."

"If Mr. Mostyn is coming home, he can ask you to Mostyn Hall. It is very near Rawdon Court."

"Yes. Fred said as soon as he had possession of the Court he could put both places into a ring fence. Then he would live at the Court. If he asks us there next summer I shall be sure to beg an invitation for you also; so I think you might deserve it by getting me one now. I don't want to go to Mostyn yet. Fred says it needs entire refurnishing, and if we come to the Court next summer, I have promised to give him my advice and help in making the place pretty and up to date. Have you seen Mostyn Hall?"

"I have passed it several times. It is a large, gloomy-looking place I was going to say haunted-looking. It stands in a grove of yew trees."

"So you are not going to ask me to Rawdon Court?"

"I really cannot, Dora. It is not my house. I am only a guest there."

"Never mind. Make no more excuses. I see how it is. You always were jealous of Fred's liking for me. And of course when he goes down to Mostyn you would prefer me to be absent."

"Good-by, Dora! I have a deal of shopping to do, and there is not much time before the ball, for many things will be to make."

"The ball! What ball?"

"Only one at Rawdon Court. The neighbors have been exceedingly kind to us, and the Squire is going to give a dinner and ball on the first of August."

"Sit down and tell me about the neighbors—and the ball."

"I cannot. I promised Ruth to be back at five. Our modiste is to see us at that hour."

"So Ruth is with you! Why did she not call on me?"

"Did you think I should come to London alone? And Ruth did not call because she was too busy."

"Everyone and everything comes before me now. I used to be first of all. I wish I were in Newport with dad and mamma; even Bryce would be a comfort."

"As I said before, you have Mr. Stanhope."

"Are you going to send for me to the ball?"

"I cannot promise that, Dora. Good-by."

Dora did not answer. She buried her face in the soft pillow, and Ethel closed the door to the sound of her sobs. But they did not cause her to return or to make any foolish promises. She divined their insincerity and their motive, and had no mind to take any part in forwarding the latter.

And Ruth assured her she had acted wisely. "If trouble should ever come of this friendship," she said, "Dora would very likely complain that you had always thrown Mostyn in her way, brought him to her house in New York, and brought her to him at Rawdon, in England. Marriage is such a risk, Ethel, but to marry without the courage to adapt oneself. AH!"

"You think that condition unspeakably hard?"

"There are no words for it."

"Dora was not reticent, I assure you."

"I am sorry. A wife's complaints are self-inflicted wounds;

scattered seeds, from which only misery can spring. I hope you will not see her again at this time."

"I made no promise to do so."

"And where all is so uncertain, we had better suppose all is right than that all is wrong. Even if there was the beginning of wrong, it needs but an accident to prevent it, and there are so many."

"Accidents!"

"Yes, for accident is God's part in affairs. We call it accident; it would be better to say an interposition."

"Dora told me Mostyn intended to buy Rawdon Court in September, and he has even invited the Stanhopes to stay there next summer."

"What did you say?"

"Nothing against it."

"Very good. Do you think Mostyn is in London now?"

"I should not wonder. I am sure Dora is expecting him."

In fact, the next morning they met Dora and Basil Stanhope, driving in Hyde Park with Mostyn, but the smiling greeting which passed between the parties did not, except in the case of Basil Stanhope, fairly represent the dominant feeling of anyone. As for Stanhope, his nature was so clear and truthful that he would hardly have comprehended a smile which was intended to veil feelings not to be called either quite friendly or quite pleasant. After this meeting all the joy went out of Ruth and Ethel's shopping. They wanted to get back to the

Court, and they attended strictly to business in order to do so.

Mostyn followed them very quickly. He was exceedingly anxious to see and hear for himself how his affairs regarding Rawdon stood. They were easily made plain to him, and he saw with a pang of disappointment that all his hopes of being Squire of Rawdon Manor were over. Every penny he could righteously claim was paid to him, and on the title deeds of the ancient place he had no longer the shadow of a claim. The Squire looked ten years younger as he affectionately laid both hands on the redeemed parchments, and Mostyn with enforced politeness congratulated him on their integrity and then made a hurried retreat. Of its own kind this disappointment was as great as the loss of Dora. He could think of neither without a sense of immeasurable and disastrous failure. One petty satisfaction regarding the payment of the mortgage was his only comfort. He might now show McLean that it was not want of money that had made him hitherto shy of "the good investments" offered him. He had been sure McLean in their last interview had thought so, and had, indeed, felt the half-veiled contempt with which the rich young man had expressed his pity for Mostyn's inability to take advantage at the right moment of an exceptional chance to play the game of beggaring his neighbor. Now, he told himself, he would show McLean and his braggart set that good birth and old family was for once allied with plenty of money, and he also promised his wounded sensibilities some very desirable reprisals, every one of which he felt fully competent to take.

It was, after all, a poor compensation, but there was also the gold. He thanked his father that day for the great thoughtfulness and care with which he had amassed this sum for him, and he tried to console himself with the belief that gold answered all purposes, and that the yellow metal was a better possession than the house and lands which he had longed for with an inherited and insensate craving.

Two days after this event Ethel, at her father's direction, signed a number of papers, and when that duty was completed, the Squire rose from his chair, kissed her hands and her cheeks, and in a voice full of tenderness and pride said, "I pay my respects to the future lady of Rawdon Manor, and I thank God for permitting me to see this hour. Most welcome, Lady Ethel, to the rights you inherit, and the rights you have bought." It was a moment hardly likely to be duplicated in any life, and Ethel escaped from its tense emotions as soon as possible. She could not speak, her heart was too full of joy and wonder. There are souls that say little and love much. How blessed are they!

On the following morning the invitations were sent for the dinner and dance, but the time was put forward to the eighth of August. In everyone's heart there was a hope that before that day Mostyn would have left Rawdon, but the hope was barely mentioned. In the meantime he came and went between Mostyn and Rawdon as he desired, and was received with that modern politeness which considers it best to ignore offenses that our grandfathers and grandmothers would have held for strict account and punishment.

It was evident that he had frequent letters from Dora. He knew all her movements, and spoke several times of opening Mostyn Hall and inviting the Stanhopes to stay with him until their return to America. But as this suggestion did not bring from any member of the Rawdon family the invitation hoped for, it was not acted upon. He told himself the expense would be great, and the Hall, in spite of all he could do in the interim, would look poor and shabby compared with Rawdon Court; so he put aside the proposal on the ground that he could not persuade his aunt to do the entertaining necessary. And for all the irritation and humiliations centering round his

Amelia E. Barr

loss of Rawdon and his inabilities with regard to Dora he blamed Ethel. He was sure if he had been more lovable and encouraging he could have married her, and thus finally reached Rawdon Court; and then, with all the unreason imaginable, nursed a hearty dislike to her because she would not understand his desires, and provide means for their satisfaction. The bright, joyous girl with her loving heart, her abounding vitality, and constant cheerfulness, made him angry. In none of her excellencies he had any share, conesquently he hated her.

He would have quickly returned to London, but Dora and her husband were staying with the Stanhopes, and her letters from Stanhope Castle were lachrymose complaints of the utter weariness and dreariness of life there the preaching and reading aloud, the regular walking and driving—all the innocent method of lives which recognized they were here for some higher purpose than mere physical enjoyment. And it angered Mostyn that neither Ruth nor Ethel felt any sympathy for Dora's ennui, and proposed no means of releasing her from it. He considered them both disgustingly selfish and ill-natured, and was certain that all their reluctance at Dora's presence arose from their jealousy of her beauty and her enchanting grace.

On the afternoon of the day preceding the intended entertainment Ruth, Ethel, and the Squire were in the great dining-room superintending its decoration. They were merrily laughing and chatting, and were not aware of the arrival of any visitors until Mrs. Nicholas Rawdon's rosy, good-natured face appeared at the open door. Everyone welcomed her gladly, and the Squire offered her a seat.

"Nay, Squire," she said, "I'm come to ask a favor, and I won't sit till I know whether I get it or not; for if I don't get it, I shall say good-by as quickly as I can. Our John Thomas came home this morning and his friend with him, and I want invitations for the young men, both of them. My great pleasure lies that way—if you'll give it to me."

"Most gladly," answered the Squire, and Ethel immediately went for the necessary passports. When she returned she found Mrs. Nicholas helping Ruth and the Squire to arrange the large silver and cut crystal on the sideboard, and talking at the same time with unabated vivacity.

"Yes," she was saying, "the lads would have been here two days ago, but they stayed in London to see some American lady married. John Thomas's friend knew her. She was married at the Ambassador's house. A fine affair enough, but it bewilders me this taking up marriage without priest or book. It's a new commission. The Church's warrant, it seems, is out of date. It may be right' it may be legal, but I told John Thomas if he ever got himself married in that kind of a way, he wouldn't have father or me for witnesses."

"I am glad," said the Squire, "that the young men are home in time for our dance. The young like such things."

"To be sure they do. John Thomas wouldn't give me a moment's rest till I came here. I didn't want to come. I thought John Thomas should come himself, and I told him plainly that I was ready to do anyone a favor if I could, but if he wanted me to come because he was afraid to come himself, I was just as ready to shirk the journey. And he laughed and said he was not feared for any woman living, but he did want to make his first appearance in his best clothes—and that was natural, wasn't it? So I came for the two lads." Then she looked at the girls with a smile, and said in a comfortable kind of way: "You'll find them very nice lads, indeed. I can speak for John Thomas, I have taken his measure long since; and as far as I can judge his friend,

Nature went about some full work when she made a man of him. He's got a sweet temper, and a strong mind, and a straight judgment, if I know anything about men—which Nicholas sometimes makes me think I don't. But Nicholas isn't an ordinary man, he's what you call 'an exception.'" Then shaking her head at Ethel, she continued reprovingly: "You were neither of you in church Sunday. I know some young women who went to the parish church—Methodists they are—specially to see your new hats. There's some talk about them, I can tell you, and the village milliner is pestered to copy them. She keeps her eyes open for you. You disappointed a lot of people. You ought to go to church in the country. It's the most respectable thing you can do."

"We were both very tired," said Ruth, "and the sun was hot, and we had a good Sabbath at home. Ethel read the Psalms, Epistle and Gospel for the day, and the Squire gave us some of the grandest organ music I ever heard."

"Well, well! Everyone knows the Squire is a grand player. I don't suppose there is another to match him in the whole world, and the old feeling about church-going is getting slack among the young people. They serve God now very much at their ease."

"Is not that better than serving Him on compulsion?" asked Ruth.

"I dare say. I'm no bigot. I was brought up an Independent, and went to their chapel until I married Nicholas Rawdon. My father was a broad-thinking man. He never taught me to locate God in any building; and I'm sure I don't believe our parish church is His dwelling-place. If it is, they ought to mend the roof and put a new carpet down and make things cleaner and more respectable. Well, Squire, you have silver enough to tempt all the rogues in Yorkshire, and there's a lot of them. But now I've seen it, I'll go home with these bits of paper. I shall be a very important woman to-night. Them two lads won't know how to fleech and flatter me enough. I'll be waited on hand and foot. And Nicholas will get a bit of a set-down. He was bragging about Miss Ethel bringing his invitation to his hand and promising to dance with him. I wouldn't do it if I were Miss Ethel. She'll find out, if she does, what it means to dance with a man that weighs twenty stone, and who has never turned hand nor foot to anything but money-making for thirty years."

She went away with a sweep and a rustle of her shimmering silk skirt, and left behind her such an atmosphere of hearty good-nature as made the last rush and crowd of preparations easily ordered and quickly accomplished. Before her arrival there had been some doubt as to the weather. She brought the shining sun with her, and when he set, he left them with the promise of a splendid to-morrow—a promise amply redeemed when the next day dawned. Indeed, the sunshine was so brilliant, the garden so gay and sweet, the lawn so green and firm, the avenues so shady and full of wandering songs, that it was resolved to hold the preliminary reception out of doors. Ethel and Ruth were to receive on the lawn, and at the open hall door the Squire would wait to welcome his guests.

Soon after five o'clock there was a brilliant crowd wandering and resting in the pleasant spaces; and Ethel, wearing a diaphanously white robe and carrying a rush basket full of white carnations, was moving among them distributing the flowers. She was thus the center of a little laughing, bantering group when the Nicholas Rawdon party arrived. Nicholas remained with the Squire, Mrs. Rawdon and the young men went toward Ethel. Mrs. Rawdon made a very handsome appearance—"an aristocratic Britannia in white liberty silk and old lace," whispered Ruth, and Ethel looked up quickly, to meet her merry eyes full of some unexplained triumph. In truth, the proud mother was anticipating a great pleasure, not only in the presentation of her adored son, but also in the curiosity and astonishment she felt sure would be evoked by his friend. So, with the boldness of one who brings happy tidings, she pressed forward. Ethel saw her approach, and went to meet her. Suddenly her steps were arrested. An extraordinary thing was going to happen. The Apollo of her dreams, the singer of the Holland House pavement, was at Mrs. Rawdon's side, was talking to her, was evidently a familiar friend. She was going to meet him, to speak to him at last. She would hear his name in a few moments; all that she had hoped and believed was coming true. And the clear, resonant voice of Lydia Rawdon was like music in her ears as she said, with an air of triumph she could not hide:

"Miss Rawdon, I want you to know my son, Mr. John Thomas Rawdon, and also John Thomas's cousin, Mr. Tyrrel Rawdon, of the United States." Then Mr. Tyrrel Rawdon looked into Ethel's face, and in that marvelous meeting of their eyes, swift as the firing of a gun, their pupils dilated and flashed with recognition, and the blood rushed crimson over both faces. She gave the gentlemen flowers, and listened to Mrs. Rawdon's chatter, and said in reply she knew not what. A swift and exquisite excitement had followed her surprise. Feelings she could not voice were beating at her lips, and yet she knew that without her conscious will she had expressed her astonishment and pleasure. It was, indeed, doubtful whether any after speech or explanation would as clearly satisfy both hearts as did that momentary flash from soul to soul of mutual remembrance and interest.

"I thought I'd give you a surprise," said Mrs. Rawdon delightedly. "You didn't know the Tyrrel-Rawdons had a branch in America, did you? We are a bit proud of them, I can tell you that."

And, indeed, the motherly lady had some reason. John Thomas was a handsome youth of symmetrical bone and flesh and well-developed muscle. He had clear, steady, humorous eyes; a manner frank and independent, not to be put upon; and yet Ethel divined, though she could not have declared, the "want" in his appearance—that all-overish grace and elasticity which comes only from the development of the brain and nervous system. His face was also marred by the seal of commonness which trade impresses on so many men, the result of the subjection of the intellect to the will, and of the impossibility of grasping things except as they relate to self. In this respect the American cousin was his antipodes. His whole body had a psychical expression—slim, elastic, alert. Over his bright gray eyes the eyelids drew themselves horizontally, showing his dexterity and acuteness of mind; indeed, his whole expression and mien

"Were, as are the eagle's keen,
All the man was aquiline."

These personal characteristics taking some minutes to describe were almost an instantaneous revelation to Ethel, for what the soul sees it sees in a flash of understanding. But at that time she only answered her impressions without any inquiry concerning them. She was absorbed by the personal presence of the men, and all that was lovely and lovable in her nature responded to their admiration.

As they strolled together through a flowery alley, she made them pass their hands through the thyme and lavender, and listen to a bird singing its verses, loud and then soft, in the scented air above them. They came out where the purple plums and golden apricots were beginning to brighten a southern wall, and there, moodily walking by himself, they met Mostyn face to face. An angry flash and movement interpreted his annoyance, but he immediately recovered himself, and met Ethel and his late political opponent with polite equanimity. But a decided constraint fell on the happy party, and Ethel was relieved to hear the first tones of the great bell swing out from its lofty tower the call to the dining-room.

As far as Mostyn was concerned, this first malapropos meeting indicated the whole evening. His heart was beating quickly to some sense of defeat which he did not take the trouble to analyze. He only saw the man who had shattered his political hopes and wasted his money in possession also of what he thought he might rightly consider his place at Ethel's side. He had once contemplated making Ethel his bride, and though the matrimonial idea had collapsed as completely as the political one, the envious, selfish misery of the "dog in the manger" was eating at his heartstrings. He did not want Ethel; but oh, how he hated the thought of either John Thomas or that American Raw-don winning her! His seat at the dinner-table also annoyed him. It was far enough from the objects of his resentment to prevent him hearing or interfering in their merry conversation; and he told himself with passionate indignation that Ethel had never once in all their intercourse been so beautiful and bright as she revealed herself that evening to those two Rawdon youths—one a mere loom-master, the other an American whom no one knew anything about.

The long, bewitching hours of the glorious evening added fuel to the flame of his anger. He could only procure from Ethel the promise of one unimportant dance at the close of her programme; and the American had three dances, and the mere loom-man two. And though he attempted to restore his self-complacency by devoting his whole attentions to the only titled young ladies in the room, he had throughout the evening a sense of being snubbed, and of being a person no longer of much importance at Rawdon Court. And the reasoning of wounded self-love is a singular process. Mostyn was quite oblivious of any personal cause for the change; he attributed it entirely to the Squire's ingratitude.

"I did the Squire a good turn when he needed it, and of course he hates me for the obligation; and as for the Judge and his fine daughter, they interfered with my business—did me a great wrong—and they are only illustrating the old saying, 'Since I wronged you I never liked you.'" After indulging such thoughts awhile, he resolved to escort the ladies Aurelia and Isolde Danvers to Danvers Castle, and leave Miss Ethel to find a partner for her last dance, a decision that favored John Thomas, greatly relieved Ethel, and bestowed upon himself that most irritating of all punishments, a self-inflicted disappointment.

This evening was the inauguration of a period of undimmed delight. In it the Tyrrel-Rawdons concluded a firm and affectionate alliance with the elder branch at the Court, and one day after a happy family dinner John Thomas made the startling proposal that "the portrait of the disinherited, disowned Tyrrel should be restored to its place in the family gallery." He said he had "just walked through it, and noticed that the spot was still vacant, and I think surely," he added, "the young man's father must have meant to recall him home some day, but perhaps death took him unawares."

"Died in the hunting-field," murmured the Squire.

John Thomas bowed his head to the remark, and proceeded, "So perhaps, Squire, it may be in your heart to forgive the dead, and bring back the poor lad's picture to its place. They who sin for love aren't so bad, sir, as they who sin for money. I never heard worse of Tyrrel Rawdon than that he loved a poor woman instead of a rich woman—and married her. Those that have gone before us into the next life, I should think are good friends together; and I wouldn't wonder if we might even make them happier there if we conclude to forget all old wrongs and live together here—as Rawdons ought to live—like one family."

"I am of your opinion, John Thomas," said the Squire, rising, and as he did so he looked at the Judge, who immediately indorsed the proposal. One after the other rose with sweet and strong assent, until there was only Tyrrel Rawdon's voice lacking. But when all had spoken he rose also, and said:

"I am Tyrrel Rawdon's direct descendant, and I speak for him when I say to-day, 'Make room for me among my kindred!' He that loves much may be forgiven much."

Then the housekeeper was called, and they went slowly, with soft words, up to the third story of the house. And the room unused for a century was flung wide open; the shutters were unbarred, and the sunshine flooded it; and there amid his fishing tackle, guns, and whips, and faded ballads upon the wall, and books of wood lore and botany, and dress suits of velvet and satin, and hunting suits of scarlet—all faded and falling to pieces—stood the picture of Tyrrel Rawdon, with its face turned to the wall. The Squire made a motion to his descendant, and the young American tenderly turned it to the light. There was no decay on those painted lineaments. The almost boyish face, with its loving eyes and laughing mouth, was still twenty-four years old; and with a look of pride and affection the Squire lifted the picture and placed it in the hands of the Tyrrel Rawdon of the day.

The hanging of the picture in its old place was a silent and tender little ceremony, and after it the party separated. Mrs.

Rawdon went with Ruth to rest a little. She said "she had a headache," and she also wanted a good womanly talk over the affair. The Squire, Judge Rawdon, Mr. Nicholas Rawdon, and John Thomas returned to the dining-room to drink a bottle of such mild Madeira as can only now be found in the cellars of old county magnates, and Ethel and Tyrrel Rawdon strolled into the garden. There had not been in either mind any intention of leaving the party, but as they passed through the hall Tyrrel saw Ethel's garden hat and white parasol lying on a table, and, impelled by some sudden and unreasoned instinct, he offered them to her. Not a word of request was spoken; it was the eager, passionate command of his eyes she obeyed. And for a few minutes they were speechless, then so intensely conscious that words stumbled and were lame, and they managed only syllables at a time. But he took her hand, and they came by sunny alleys of boxwood to a great plane tree, bearing at wondrous height a mighty wealth of branches. A bank of soft, green turf encircled its roots, and they sat down in the trembling shadows. It was in the midst of the herb garden; beds of mint and thyme, rosemary and marjoram, basil, lavender, and other fragrant plants were around, and close at hand a little city of straw skeps peopled by golden brown bees; From these skeps came a delicious aroma of riced flowers and virgin wax. It was a new Garden of Eden, in which life was sweet as perfume and pure as prayer. Nothing stirred the green, sunny afternoon but the murmur of the bees, and the sleepy twittering of the birds in the plane branches. An inexpressible peace swept like the breath of heaven through the odorous places. They sat down sighing for very happiness. The silence became too eloquent. At length it was almost unendurable, and Ethel said softly:

"How still it is!"

Tyrrel looked at her steadily with beaming eyes. Then he took from his pocket a little purse of woven gold and

Amelia E. Barr

opal-tinted beads, and held it in his open hand for her to see, watching the bright blush that spread over her face, and the faint, glad smile that parted her lips.

"You understand?"

"Yes. It is mine."

"It was yours. It is now mine."

"How did you get it?"

"I bought it from the old man you gave it to."

"Oh! Then you know him? How is that?"

"The hotel people sent a porter home with him lest he should be robbed. Next day I made inquiries, and this porter told me where he lived. I went there and bought this purse from him. I knew some day it would bring me to you. I have carried it over my heart ever since."

"So you noticed me?"

"I saw you all the time I was singing. I have never forgotten you since that hour."

"What made you sing?"

"Compassion, fate, an urgent impulse; perhaps, indeed, your piteous face—I saw it first."

"Really?"

"I saw it first. I saw it all the time I was singing. When you dropped this purse my soul met yours in a moment's greeting. It was a promise. I knew I should meet you again. I have loved you ever since. I wanted to tell you so the hour we met. It has been hard to keep my secret so long."

"It was my secret also."

"I love you beyond all words. My life is in your hands. You can make me the gladdest of mortals. You can send me away forever."

"Oh, no, I could not! I could not do that!" The rest escapes words; but thus it was that on this day of days these two came by God's grace to each other.

> For all things come by fate to flower,
> At their unconquerable hour.

And the very atmosphere of such bliss is diffusive; it seemed as if all the living creatures around understood. In the thick, green branches the birds began to twitter the secret, and certainly the wise, wise bees knew also, in some occult way, of the love and joy that had just been revealed. A wonderful humming and buzzing filled the hives, and the air vibrated with the movement of wings. Some influence more swift and secret than the birds of the air carried the matter further, for it finally reached Royal, the Squire's favorite collie, who came sauntering down the alley, pushed his nose twice under Ethel's elbow, and then with a significant look backward, advised the lovers to follow him to the house.

When they finally accepted his invitation, they found Mrs. Rawdon drinking a cup of tea with Ruth in the hall. Ethel joined them with affected high spirits and random explanations and excuses, but both women no-ticed her radiant face and exulting air. "The garden is such a heavenly place," she said ecstatically, and Mrs Rawdon remarked, as she rose

Amelia E. Barr

and put her cup on the table, "Girls need chaperons in gardens if they need them anywhere. I made Nicholas Rawdon a promise in Mossgill Garden I've had to spend all my life since trying to keep."

"Tyrrel and I have been sitting under the plane tree watching the bees. They are such busy, sensible creatures."

"They are that," answered Mrs. Rawdon. "If you knew all about them you would wonder a bit. My father had a great many; he studied their ways and used to laugh at the ladies of the hive being so like the ladies of the world. You see the young lady bees are just as inexperienced as a schoolgirl. They get lost in the flowers, and are often so overtaken and reckless, that the night finds them far from the hive, heavy with pollen and chilled with cold. Sometimes father would lift one of these imprudent young things, carry it home, and try to get it admitted. He never could manage it. The lady bees acted just as women are apt to do when other women GO where they don't go, or DO as they don't do."

"But this is interesting," said Ruth. "Pray, how did the ladies of the hive behave to the culprit?"

"They came out and felt her all over, turned her round and round, and then pushed her out of their community. There was always a deal of buzzing about the poor, silly thing, and I shouldn't wonder if their stings were busy too. Bees are ill-natured as they can be. Well, well, I don't blame anyone for sitting in the garden such a day as this; only, as I was saying, gardens have been very dangerous places for women as far as I know."

Ruth laughed softly. "I shall take a chaperon with me, then, when I go into the garden."

"I would, dearie. There's the Judge; he's a very suitable, sedate-looking one but you never can tell. The first woman found in a garden and a tree had plenty of sorrow for herself and every woman that has lived after her. I wish Nicholas and John Thomas would come. I'll warrant they're talking what they call politics."

Politics was precisely the subject which had been occupying them, for when Tyrrel entered the dining-room, the Squire, Judge Rawdon, and Mr. Nicholas Rawdon were all standing, evidently just finishing a Conservative argument against the Radical opinions of John Thomas. The young man was still sitting, but he rose with smiling good-humor as Tyrrel entered.

"Here is Cousin Tyrrel," he cried; "he will tell you that you may call a government anything you like radical, conservative, republican, democratic, socialistic, but if it isn't a CHEAP government, it isn't a good government; and there won't be a cheap government in England till poor men have a deal to say about making laws and voting taxes."

"Is that the kind of stuff you talk to our hands, John Thomas? No wonder they are neither to hold nor to bind."

They were in the hall as John Thomas finished his political creed, and in a few minutes the adieux were said, and the wonderful day was over. It had been a wonderful day for all, but perhaps no one was sorry for a pause in life—a pause in which they might rest and try to realize what it had brought and what it had taken away. The Squire went at once to his room, and Ethel looked at Ruth inquiringly. She seemed exhausted, and was out of sympathy with all her surroundings.

"What enormous vitality these Yorkshire women must have!" she said almost crossly. "Mrs. Rawdon has been talking incessantly for six hours. She has felt all she said. She has frequently risen and walked about. She has used all sorts of actions to emphasize her words, and she is as fresh as if she had just taken her morning bath. How do the men stand them?"

"Because they are just as vital. John Thomas will overlook and scold and order his thousand hands all day, talk even his mother down while he eats his dinner, and then lecture or lead his Musical Union, or conduct a poor man's concert, or go to 'the Weaver's Union,' and what he calls 'threep them' for two or three hours that labor is ruining capital, and killing the goose that lays golden eggs for them. Oh, they are a wonderful race, Ruth!"

"I really can't discuss them now, Ethel."

"Don't you want to know what Tyrrel said to me this afternoon?"

"My dear, I know. Lovers have said such things before, and lovers will say them evermore. You shall tell me in the morning. I thought he looked distrait and bored with our company."

Indeed, Tyrrel was so remarkably quiet that John Thomas also noticed his mood, and as they sat smoking in Tyrrel's room, he resolved to find out the reason, and with his usual directness asked:

"What do you think of Ethel Rawdon, Tyrrel,"

"I think she is the most beautiful woman I ever saw. She has also the most sincere nature, and her high spirit is sweetly tempered by her affectionate heart."

"I am glad you know so much about her. Look here, Cousin Tyrrel, I fancied to-night you were a bit jealous of me. It is easy to see you are in love, and I've no doubt you were thinking of the days when you would be thousands of miles away, and I should have the ground clear and so on, eh?"

"Suppose I was, cousin, what then?"

"You would be worrying for nothing. I don't want to marry Ethel Rawdon. If I did, you would have to be on the ground all the time, and then I should best you; but I picked out my wife two years ago, and if we are both alive and well, we are going to be married next Christmas."

"I am delighted. I—"

"I thought you would be."

"Who is the young lady?"

"Miss Lucy Watson. Her father is the Independent minister. He is a gentleman, though his salary is less than we give our overseer. And he is a great scholar. So is Lucy. She finished her course at college this summer, and with high honors. Bless you, Tyrrel, she knows far more than I do about everything but warps and looms and such like. I admire a clever woman, and I'm proud of Lucy."

"Where is she now?"

"Well, she was a bit done up with so much study, and so she went to Scarborough for a few weeks. She has an aunt there. The sea breezes and salt water soon made her fit for anything. She may be home very soon now. Then, Tyrrel, you'll see a beauty—face like a rose, hair brown as a nut, eyes that make your heart go galloping, the most enticing mouth, the prettiest figure, and she loves me with all her heart. When she says 'John Thomas, dear one,' I tremble with pleasure, and when she lets me kiss her sweet mouth, I really don't know where I am. What would you say if a girl whispered, 'I love you, and nobody but you,' and gave you a kiss that was like—like wine and roses? Now what would you say?"

"I know as little as you do what I would say. It's a situation to make a man coin new words. I suppose your family are pleased."

"Well, I never thought about my family till I had Lucy's word. Then I told mother. She knew Lucy all through. Mother has a great respect for Independents, and though father sulked a bit at first, mother had it out with him one night, and when mother has father quiet in their room father comes to see things just as she wants him. I suppose that's the way with wives. Lucy will be just like that. She's got a sharp little temper, too. She'll let me have a bit of it, no doubt, now and then."

"Will you like that?"

"I wouldn't care a farthing for a wife without a bit of temper. There would be no fun in living with a woman of that kind. My father would droop and pine if mother didn't spur him on now and then. And he likes it. Don't I know? I've seen mother snappy and awkward with him all breakfast time, tossing her head, and rattling the china, and declaring she was worn out with men that let all the good bargains pass them; perhaps making fun of us because we couldn't manage to get along without strikes. She had no strikes with her hands, she'd like to see her women stand up and talk to her about shorter hours, and so on; and father would look at me sly-like, and as we walked to the mill together he'd laugh contentedly and say, 'Your mother was quite refreshing this morning, John Thomas. She has keyed me up to a right pitch. When Jonathan Arkroyd comes about that wool he sold us I'll be all ready for him.' So you see I'm not against a sharp temper. I like women as Tennyson says English girls are, 'roses set round with little wilful thorns,' eh?"

Unusual as this conversation was, its general tone was assumed by Ethel in her confidential talk with Ruth the following day. Of course, Ruth was not at all surprised at the news Ethel brought her, for though the lovers had been individually sure they had betrayed their secret to no one, it had really been an open one to Ruth since the hour of their meeting. She was sincerely ardent in her praises of Tyrrel Rawdon, but—and there is always a but—she wondered if Ethel had "noticed what a quick temper he had."

"Oh, yes," answered Ethel, "I should not like him not to have a quick temper. I expect my husband to stand up at a moment's notice for either mine or his own rights or opinions."

And in the afternoon when all preliminaries had been settled and approved, Judge Rawdon expressed himself in the same manner to Ruth. "Yes," he said, in reply to her timid suggestion of temper, "you can strike fire anywhere with him if you try it, but he has it under control. Besides, Ethel is just as quick to flame up. It will be Rawdon against Rawdon, and Ethel's weapons are of finer, keener steel than Tyrrel's. Ethel will hold her own. It is best so."

"How did the Squire feel about such a marriage?"

"He was quite overcome with delight. Nothing was said to Tyrrel about Ethel having bought the reversion of Rawdon Manor, for things have been harder to get into proper shape than I thought they would be, and it may be another month before all is finally settled; but the Squire has the secret satisfaction, and he was much affected by the certainty of a Rawdon at Rawdon Court after him. He declined to think of it in any other way but 'providential,' and of course I let him take all the satisfaction he could out of the idea. Ever since he heard of the engagement he has been at the organ singing the One Hundred and Third Psalm."

"He is the dearest and noblest of men. How soon shall we go home now?"

"In about a month. Are you tired of England?"

"I shall be glad to see America again. There was a letter from Dora this morning. They sail on the twenty-third."

"Do you know anything of Mostyn?"

"Since he wrote us a polite farewell we have heard nothing."

"Do you think he went to America?"

"I cannot tell. When he bid us good-by he made no statement as to his destination; he merely said 'he was leaving England on business.'"

"Well, Ruth, we shall sail as soon as I am satisfied all is right. There is a little delay about some leases and other matters. In the meantime the lovers are in Paradise wherever we locate them."

And in Paradise they dwelt for another four weeks. The ancient garden had doubtless many a dream of love to keep, but none sweeter or truer than the idyl of Tyrrel and Ethel Rawdon. They were never weary of rehearsing it; every incident of its growth had been charming and romantic, and, as they believed, appointed from afar. As the summer waxed hotter the beautiful place took on an appearance of royal color and splendor, and the air was languid with the perfume of the clove carnations and tall white August lilies. Fluted dahlias, scarlet poppies, and all the flowers that exhale their spice in the last hot days of August burned incense for them. Their very hair was laden with odor, their fingers flower-sweet, their minds took on the many colors of their exquisite surroundings.

And it was part of this drama of love and scent and color that they should see it slowly assume the more ethereal loveliness of September, and watch the subtle amber rays shine through the thinning boughs, and feel that all nature was becoming idealized. The birds were then mostly silent. They had left their best notes on the hawthorns and among the roses; but the crickets made a cheerful chirrup, and the great brown butterflies displayed their richest velvets, and the gossamer-like insects in the dreamy atmosphere performed dances and undulations full of grace and mystery. And all these marvelous changes imparted to love that sweet sadness which is beyond all words poetic and enchaining.

Yet however sweet the hours, they pass away, and it is not much memory can save from the mutable, happy days of love. Still, when the hour of departure came they had garnered enough to sweeten all the after-straits and stress of time. September had then perceptibly begun to add to the nights and shorten the days, and her tender touch had been laid on everything. With a smile and a sigh the Rawdons turned their faces to their pleasant home in the Land of the West. It was to be but a short farewell. They had promised the Squire to return the following summer, but he felt the desolation of the parting very keenly. With his hat slightly lifted above his white head, he stood watching them out of

Amelia E. Barr

sight. Then he went to his organ, and very soon grand waves of melody rolled outward and upward, and blended themselves with the clear, soaring voice of Joel, the lad who blew the bellows of the instrument, and shared all his master's joy in it. They played and sang until the Squire rose weary, but full of gladness. The look of immortality was in his eyes, its sure and certain hope in his heart. He let Joel lead him to his chair by the window, and then he said to himself with visible triumph:

"What Mr. Spencer or anyone else writes about 'the Unknowable' I care not. I KNOW IN WHOM I have believed. Joel, sing that last sequence again. Stand where I can see thee." And the lad's joyful voice rang exulting out:

"Lord, Thou hast been our dwelling-place in all generations. Before the mountains were brought forth, or ever Thou hadst formed the world, from everlasting to everlasting Thou art God! Thou art God! Thou art God!"

"That will do, Joel. Go thy ways now. Lord, Thou hast been our dwelling-place in all generations. 'Unknowable,' Thou hast been our dwelling-place in all generations. No, no, no, what an ungrateful sinner I would be to change the Lord everlasting for the Unknowable.'"

CHAPTER IX

NEW YORK is at its very brightest and best in October. This month of the year may be safely trusted not to disappoint. The skies are blue, the air balmy, and there is generally a delightful absence of wind. The summer exiles are home again from Jersey boarding houses, and mountain camps, and seaside hotels, and thankful to the point of hilarity that this episode of the year is over, that they can once more dwell under their own roofs without breaking any of the manifest laws of the great goddess Custom or Fashion.

Judge Rawdon's house had an especially charming "at home" appearance. During the absence of the family it had been made beautiful inside and outside, and the white stone, the plate glass, and falling lace evident to the street, had an almost conscious look of luxurious propriety.

The Judge frankly admitted his pleasure in his home surroundings. He said, as they ate their first meal in the familiar room, that "a visit to foreign countries was a grand, patriotic tonic." He vowed that the "first sight of the Stars and Stripes at Sandy Hook had given him the finest emotion he had ever felt in his life," and was altogether in his proudest American mood. Ruth sympathized with him. Ethel listened smiling. She knew well that the English strain had only temporarily exhausted itself; it would have its period of revival at the proper time.

"I am going to see grandmother," she said gayly. "I shall stay with her all day."

"But I have a letter from her," interrupted the Judge, "and she will not return home until next week."

"I am sorry. I was anticipating so eagerly the joy of seeing her. Well, as I cannot do so, I will go and call on Dora Stanhope."

"I would not if I were you, Ethel," said Ruth. "Let her come and call on you."

"I had a little note from her this morning, welcoming me home, and entreating me to call."

The Judge rose as Ethel was speaking, and no more was said about the visit at that time but a few hours later Ethel came down from her room ready for the street and frankly told Ruth she had made up her mind to call on Dora.

"Then I will only remind you, Ethel, that Dora is not a fortunate woman to know. As far as I can see, she is one of those who sow pain of heart and vexation of spirit about every house they enter, even their own. But I cannot gather experience for you, it will have to grow in your own garden."

"All right, dear Ruth, and if I do not like its growth, I will pull it up by the roots, I assure you."

Ruth went with her to the door and watched her walk leisurely down the broad steps to the street. The light kindled in her eyes and on her face as she did so. She already felt the magnetism of the great city, and with a laughing farewell walked rapidly toward Dora's house.

Her card brought an instant response, and she heard Dora's welcome before the door was opened. And her first greeting was an enthusiastic compliment, "How beautiful you have grown, Ethel!" she cried. "Ah, that is the European finish. You have gained it, my dear; you really are very much improved."

"And you also, Dora?"

The words were really a question, but Dora accepted them as an assertion, and was satisfied.

"I suppose I am," she answered, "though I'm sure I can't tell how it should be so, unless worry of all kinds is good for good looks. I've had enough of that for a lifetime."

"Now, Dora."

"Oh, it's the solid truth—partly your fault too."

"I never interfered—"

"Of course you didn't, but you ought to have interfered. When you called on me in London you might have seen that I was not happy; and I wanted to come to Rawdon Court, and you would not invite me. I called your behavior then 'very mean,' and I have not altered my opinion of it."

"There were good reasons, Dora, why I could not ask you."

"Good reasons are usually selfish ones, Ethel, and Fred Mostyn told me what they were.

"He likely told you untruths, Dora, for he knew nothing

about my reasons. I saw very little of him."

"I know. You treated him as badly as you treated me, and all for some wild West creature—a regular cowboy, Fred said, but then a Rawdon!"

"Mr. Mostyn has misrepresented Mr. Tyrrel Rawdon—that is all about it. I shall not explain 'how' or 'why.' Did you enjoy yourself at Stanhope Castle?"

"Enjoy myself! Are you making fun of me? Ethel, dear, it was the most awful experience. You never can imagine such a life, and such women. They were dressed for a walk at six o'clock; they had breakfast at half-past seven. They went to the village and inspected cottages, and gave lessons in housekeeping or dressmaking or some other drudgery till noon. They walked back to the Castle for lunch. They attended to their own improvement from half-past one until four, had lessons in drawing and chemistry, and, I believe, electricity. They had another walk, and then indulged themselves with a cup of tea. They dressed and received visitors, and read science or theology between whiles. There was always some noted preacher or scholar at the dinner table. The conversation was about acids and explosives, or the planets or bishops, or else on the never, never-ending subject of elevating the workingman and building schools for his children. Basil, of course, enjoyed it. He thought he was giving me a magnificent object lesson. He was never done praising the ladies Mary Elinor and Adelaide Stanhope. I'm sure I wish he had married one or all of them—and I told him so."

"You could not be so cruel, Dora."

"I managed it with the greatest ease imaginable. He was always trotting at their side. They spoke of him as 'the most pious young man.' I have no doubt they were all in love with him. I hope they were. I used to pretend to be very much in love when they were present. I dare say it made them wretched. Besides, they blushed and thought me improper. Basil didn't approve, either, so I hit all round."

She rose at this memory and shook out her silk skirts, and walked up and down the room with an air that was the visible expression of the mockery and jealousy in her heart. This was an entirely different Dora to the lachrymose, untidy wife at the Savoy Hotel in London, and Ethel had a momentary pang at the thought of the suffering which was responsible for the change.

"If I had thought, Dora, you were so uncomfortable, I would have asked Basil and you to the Court."

"You saw I was not happy when I was at the Savoy."

"I thought you and Basil had had a kind of lovers' quarrel, and that it would blow over in an hour or two; no one likes to meddle with an affair of that kind. Are you going to Newport, or is Mrs. Denning in New York?"

"That is another trouble, Ethel. When I wrote mother I wanted to come to her, she sent me word she was going to Lenox with a friend. Then, like you, she said 'she had no liberty to invite me,' and so on. I never knew mother act in such a way before. I nearly broke my heart about it for a few days, then I made up my mind I wouldn't care."

"Mrs. Denning, I am sure, thought she did the wisest and kindest thing possible."

"I didn't want mother to be wise. I wanted her to understand that I was fairly worn out with my present life and needed a change. I'm sure she did understand. Then why was she so cruel?" and she shrugged her shoulders impatiently and sat down. "I'm so tired of life," she continued. "When did you hear of Fred Mostyn?"

"I know nothing of his movements. Is he in America?"

"Somewhere. I asked mother if he was in Newport, and she never answered the question. I suppose he will be in New York for the winter season. I hope so."

This topic threatened to be more dangerous than the other, and Ethel, after many and futile attempts to bring conversation into safe commonplace channels, pleaded other engagements and went away. She was painfully depressed by the interview. All the elements of tragedy were gathered together under the roof she had just left, and, as far as she could see, there was no deliverer wise and strong enough to prevent a calamity. She did not repeat to Ruth the conversation which had been so painful to her. She described Dora's dress and appearance, and commented on Fred Mostyn's description of Tyrrel Rawdon, and on Mrs. Denning's refusal of her daughter's proposed visit.

Ruth thought the latter circumstance significant. "I dare say Mostyn was in Newport at that time," she answered. "Mrs. Denning has some very quick perceptions." And Ruth's opinion was probably correct, for during dinner the Judge remarked in a casual manner that he had met Mr. Mostyn on the avenue as he was coming home. "He was well," he said, "and made all the usual inquiries as to your health." And both Ruth and Ethel understood that he wished them to know of Mostyn's presence in the city, and to be prepared for meeting him; but did not care to discuss the subject further, at least at that time. The information brought precisely the same thought at the same moment to both women, and as soon as they were alone they uttered it.

"She knew Mostyn was in the city," said Ethel in a low voice.

"Certainly."

"She was expecting him."

"I am sure of it."

"Her elaborate and beautiful dressing was for him."

"Poor Basil!"

"She asked me to stay and lunch with her, but very coolly, and when I refused, did not press the matter as she used to do. Yes, she was expecting him. I understand now her nervous manner, her restlessness, her indifference to my short visit. I wish I could do anything."

"You cannot, and you must not try."

"Some one must try."

"There is her husband. Have you heard from Tyrrel yet,"

"I have had a couple of telegrams. He will write from Chicago."

"Is he going at once to the Hot Springs?"

"As rapidly as possible. Colonel Rawdon is now there, and very ill. Tyrrel will put his father first of all. The trouble at the mine can be investigated afterwards."

"You will miss him very much. You have been so happy together."

"Of course I shall miss him. But it will be a good thing for us to be apart awhile. Love must have some time in which to grow. I am a little tired of being very happy, and I think Tyrrel also will find absence a relief. In 'Lalla Rookh' there is a line about love 'falling asleep in a sameness of splendor.' It might. How melancholy is a long spell of hot, sunshiny weather, and how gratefully we welcome the first shower of rain."

"Love has made you a philosopher, Ethel."

"Well, it is rather an advantage than otherwise. I am going to take a walk, Ruth, into the very heart of Broadway. I have had enough of the peace of the country. I want the crack, and crash, and rattle, and grind of wheels, the confused cries, the snatches of talk and laughter, the tread of crowds, the sound of bells, and clocks, and chimes. I long for all the chaotic, unintelligible noise of the streets. How suggestive it is! Yet it never explains itself. It only gives one a full sense of life. Love may need just the same stimulus. I wish grandmother would come home. I should not require Broadway as a stimulus. I am afraid she will be very angry with me, and there will be a battle royal in Gramercy Park."

It was nearly a week before Ethel had this crisis to meet. She went down to it with a radiant face and charming manner, and her reception was very cordial. Madam would not throw down the glove until the proper moment; besides, there were many very interesting subjects to talk over, and she wanted "to find things out" that would never be told unless tempers were propitious. Added to these reasons was the solid one that she really adored her granddaughter, and was immensely cheered by the very sight of the rosy, smiling countenance lifted to her sitting-room window in passing. She, indeed, pretended to be there in order to get a good light for her new shell pattern, but she was watching for Ethel, and Ethel understood the shell-pattern fiction very well. She had heard something similar often.

"My darling grandmother," she cried, "I thought you would never come home."

"It wasn't my fault, dear. Miss Hillis and an imbecile young doctor made me believe I had a cold. I had no cold. I had nothing at all but what I ought to have. I've been made to take all sorts of things, and do all sorts of things that I hate to take and hate to do. For ten days I've been kicking my old heels against bedclothes. Yesterday I took things in my own hands."

"Never mind, Granny dear, it was all a good discipline."

"Discipline! You impertinent young lady! Discipline for your grandmother! Discipline, indeed! That one word may cost you a thousand dollars, miss."

"I don't care if it does, only you must give the thousand dollars to poor Miss Hillis."

"Poor Miss Hillis has had a most comfortable time with me all summer."

"I know she has, consequently she will feel her comfortless room and poverty all the more after it. Give her the thousand, Granny. I'm willing."

"What kind of company have you been keeping, Ethel Rawdon? Who has taught you to squander dollars by the thousand? Discipline! I think you are giving me a little now—a thousand dollars a lesson, it seems—no wonder, after the carryings-on at Rawdon Court."

"Dear grandmother, we had the loveliest time you can imagine. And there is not, in all the world, such a noble old gentleman as Squire Percival Rawdon."

"I know all about Percival Rawdon—a proud, careless, extravagant, loose-at-ends man, dancing and singing and loving as it suited time and season, taking no thought for the future, and spending with both hands; hard on women, too, as could be."

"Grandmother, I never saw a more courteous gentleman. He worships women. He was never tired of talking about you."

"What had he to say about me?"

"That you were the loveliest girl in the county, and that he never could forget the first time he saw you. He said you were like the vision of an angel."

"Nonsense! I was just a pretty girl in a book muslin frock and a white sash, with a rose at my breast. I believe they use book muslin for linings now, but it did make the sheerest, lightest frocks any girl could want. Yes, I remember that time. I was going to a little party and crossing a meadow to shorten the walk, and Squire Percival had been out with his gun, and he laid it down and ran to help me over the stile. A handsome young fellow he was then as ever stepped in shoe leather."

"And he must have loved you dearly. He would sit hour after hour telling Ruth and me how bright you were, and how all the young beaux around Monk-Rawdon adored you."

"Nonsense! Nonsense! I had beaux to be sure. What pretty girl hasn't?"

"And he said his brother Edward won you because he was most worthy of your love."

"Well, now, I chose Edward Rawdon because he was willing to come to America. I longed to get away from Monk-Rawdon. I was faint and weary with the whole stupid place. And the idea of living a free and equal life, and not caring what lords and squires and their proud ladies said or did, pleased me wonderfully. We read about Niagara and the great prairies and the new bright cities, and Edward and I resolved to make our home there. Your grandfather wasn't a man to like being 'the Squire's brother.' He could stand alone."

"Are you glad you came to America?"

"Never sorry a minute for it. Ten years in New York is worth fifty years in Monk-Rawdon, or Rawdon Court either."

"Squire Percival was very fond of me. He thought I resembled you, grandmother, but he never admitted I was as handsome as you were."

"Well, Ethel dear, you are handsome enough for the kind of men you'll pick up in this generation—most of them bald at thirty, wearing spectacles at twenty or earlier, and in spite of the fuss they make about athletics breaking all to nervous bits about fifty."

"Grandmother, that is pure slander. I know some very fine young men, handsome and athletic both."

"Beauty is a matter of taste, and as to their athletics, they can run a mile with a blacksmith, but when the thermometer rises to eighty-five degrees it knocks them all to pieces. They sit fanning themselves like schoolgirls, and call for juleps and ice-water. I've got eyes yet, my dear. Squire Percival was a different kind of man; he could follow the hounds all day and dance all night. The hunt had not a rider like him; he balked at neither hedge, gate, nor water; a right gallant, courageous, honorable, affectionate gentleman as ever Yorkshire bred, and she's bred lots of superfine ones. What ever made him get into such a mess with his estate? Your grandfather thought him as straight as a string in money matters."

"You said just now he was careless and extravagant."

"Well, I did him wrong, and I'm sorry for it. How did he manage to need eighty thousand pounds?"

"It is rather a pitiful story, grandmother, but he never once blamed those who were in the wrong. His son for many years had been the real manager of the estate. He was a speculator; his grandsons were wild and extravagant. They began to borrow money ten years ago and had to go on."

"Whom did they borrow from?"

"Fred Mostyn's father."

"The devil! Excuse me, Ethel—but the name suits and may stand."

"The dear old Squire would have taken the fault on himself if he could have done so. They that wronged him were his own, and they were dead. He never spoke of them but with affection."

"Poor Percival! Your father told me he was now out of

Mostyn's power; he said you had saved the estate, but he gave me no particulars. How did you save it?"

"Bought it!"

"Nonsense!"

"House and lands and outlying farms and timber—everything."

Then a rosy color overspread Madam's face, her eyes sparkled, she rose to her feet, made Ethel a sweeping courtesy, and said:

"My respect and congratulations to Ethel, Lady of Rawdon Manor."

"Dear grandmother, what else could I do?"

"You did right."

"The Squire is Lord of the Manor as long as he lives. My father says I have done well to buy it. In the future, if I do not wish to keep it, Nicholas Rawdon will relieve me at a great financial advantage."

"Why didn't you let Nicholas Rawdon buy it now?"

"He would have wanted prompt possession. The Squire would have had to leave his home. It would have broken his heart."

"I dare say. He has a soft, loving heart. That isn't always a blessing. It can give one a deal of suffering. And I hear you have all been making idols of these Tyrrel-Rawdons. Fred tells me they are as vulgar a lot as can be."

"Fred lies! Excuse me, grandmother—but the word suits and may stand. Mr. Nicholas is pompous, and walks as slowly as if he had to carry the weight of his great fortune; but his manners are all right, and his wife and son are delightful. She is handsome, well dressed, and so good-hearted that her pretty county idioms are really charming. John Thomas is a man by himself—not handsome, but running over with good temper, and exceedingly clever and wide-awake. Many times I was forced to tell myself, John Thomas would make an ideal Squire of Rawdon."

"Why don't you marry him."

"He never asked me."

"What was the matter with the men?"

"He was already engaged to a very lovely young lady."

"I am glad she is a lady."

"She is also very clever. She has been to college and taken high honors, a thing I have not done."

"You might have done and overdone that caper; you were too sensible to try it. Well, I'm glad that part of the family is looking up. They had the right stuff in them, and it is a good thing for families to dwell together in unity. We have King David's word for that. My observation leads me to think it is far better for families to dwell apart, in unity. They seldom get along comfortably together."

Then Ethel related many pleasant, piquant scenes between the two families at Monk-Rawdon, and especially that one in which the room of the first Tyrrel had been opened and his likeness restored to its place in the family gallery. It touched the old lady to tears, and she murmured, "Poor lad! Poor lad! I wonder if he knows! I wonder if he knows!"

The crucial point of Ethel's revelations had not yet been revealed, but Madam was now in a gentle mood, and Ethel took the opportunity to introduce her to Tyrrel Rawdon. She was expecting and waiting for this topic, but stubbornly refused to give Ethel any help toward bringing it forward. At last, the girl felt a little anger at her pretended indifference, and said, "I suppose Fred Mostyn told you about Mr. Tyrrel Rawdon, of California?"

"Tyrrel Rawdon, of California! Pray, who may he be?"

"The son of Colonel Rawdon, of the United States Army."

"Oh, to be sure! Well, what of him?"

"I am going to marry him."

"I shall see about that."

"We were coming here together to see you, but before we left the steamer he got a telegram urging him to go at once to his father, who is very ill."

"I have not asked him to come and see me. Perhaps he will wait till I do so."

"If you are not going to love Tyrrel, you need not love me. I won't have you for a grandmother any longer."

"I did without you sixty years. I shall not live another twelve months, and I think I can manage to do without you for a granddaughter any longer."

"You cannot do without me. You would break your heart, and I should break mine." Whereupon Ethel began to cry with a passion that quite gratified the old lady. She watched her a few moments, and then said gently:

"There now, that will do. When he comes to New York bring him to see me. And don't name the man in the meantime. I won't talk about him till I've seen him. It isn't fair either way. Fred didn't like him."

"Fred likes no one but Dora Stanhope."

"Eh! What! Is that nonsense going on yet?"

Then Ethel described her last two interviews with Dora. She did this with scrupulous fidelity, making no suggestions that might prejudice the case. For she really wanted her grandmother's decision in order to frame her own conduct by it. Madam was not, however, in a hurry to give it.

"What do you think?" she asked Ethel.

"I have known Dora for many years; she has always told me everything."

"But nothing about Fred?"

"Nothing."

"Nothing to tell, perhaps?"

"Perhaps."

"Where does her excellent husband come in?"

"She says he is very kind to her in his way."

"And his way is to drag her over the world to see the cathedrals thereof, and to vary that pleasure with inspecting schools and reformatories and listening to great preachers. Upon my word, I feel sorry for the child! And I know all about such excellent people as the Stanhopes. I used to go to what they call 'a pleasant evening' with them. We sat around a big room lit with wax candles, and held improving conversation, or some one sang one or two of Mrs. Hemans' songs, like 'Passing Away' or 'He Never Smiled Again.' Perhaps there was a comic recitation, at which no one laughed, and finally we had wine and hot water—they called it 'port negus'—and tongue sandwiches and caraway cakes. My dear Ethel, I yawn now when I think of those dreary evenings. What must Dora have felt, right out of the maelstrom of New York's operas and theaters and dancing parties?"

"Still, Dora ought to try to feel some interest in the church affairs. She says she does not care a hairpin for them, and Basil feels so hurt."

"I dare say he does, poor fellow! He thinks St. Jude's Kindergarten and sewing circles and missionary societies are the only joys in the world. Right enough for Basil, but how about Dora?"

"They are his profession; she ought to feel an interest in them."

"Come now, look at the question sensibly. Did Dora's father bring his 'deals' and stock-jobbery home, and expect Dora and her mother to feel an interest in them? Do doctors tell their wives about their patients, and expect them to pay sympathizing visits? Does your father expect Ruth and yourself to listen to his cases and arguments, and visit his poor clients or make underclothing for them? Do men, in general, consider it a wife's place to interfere in their

Amelia E. Barr

profession or business?"

"Clergymen are different."

"Not at all. Preaching and philanthropy is their business. They get so much a year for doing it. I don't believe St. Jude's pays Mrs. Stanhope a red cent. There now, and if she isn't paid, she's right not to work. Amen to that!"

"Before she was married Dora said she felt a great interest in church work."

"I dare say she did. Marriage makes a deal of difference in a woman's likes and dislikes. Church work was courting-time before marriage; after marriage she had other opportunities."

"I think you might speak to Fred Mostyn—"

"I might, but it wouldn't be worth while. Be true to your friend as long as you can. In Yorkshire we stand by our friends, right or wrong, and we aren't too particular as to their being right. My father enjoyed justifying a man that everyone else was down on; and I've stood by many a woman nobody had a good word for. I was never sorry for doing it, either. I'll be going into a strange country soon, and I should not wonder if some of them that have gone there first will be ready to stand by me. We don't know what friends we'll be glad of there."

The dinner bell broke up this conversation, and Ethel during it told Madam about the cook and cooking at the Court and at Nicholas Rawdon's, where John Thomas had installed a French chef. Other domestic arrangements were discussed, and when the Judge called for his daughter at four o'clock, Madam vowed "she had spent one of the happiest days of her life."

"Ruth tells me," said the Judge, "that Dora Stanhope called for Ethel soon after she left home this morning. Ruth seems troubled at the continuance of this friendship. Have you spoken to your grandmother, Ethel, about Dora?"

"She has told me all there is to tell, I dare say," answered Madam.

"Well, mother, what do you think?"

"I see no harm in it yet awhile. It is not fair, Edward, to condemn upon likelihoods. We are no saints, sinful men and women, all of us, and as much inclined to forbidden fruit as any good Christians can be. Ethel can do as she feels about it; she's got a mind of her own, and I hope to goodness she'll not let Ruth Bayard bit and bridle it."

Going home the Judge evidently pondered this question, for he said after a lengthy silence, "Grandmother's ethics do not always fit the social ethics of this day, Ethel. She criticises people with her heart, not her intellect. You must be prudent. There is a remarkable thing called Respectability to be reckoned with remember that."

And Ethel answered, "No one need worry about Dora. Some women may show the edges of their character soiled and ragged, but Dora will be sure to have hers reputably finished with a hem of the widest propriety." And after a short silence the Judge added, almost in soliloquy, "And, moreover, Ethel,

"'There's a divinity that shapes our ends,
Rough-hew them how we will.'"

Amelia E. Barr

PART FOURTH

THE REAPING OF THE SOWING

CHAPTER X

WHEN Ethel and Tyrrel parted at the steamer they did not
expect a long separation, but Colonel Rawdon never
recovered his health, and for many excellent reasons Tyrrel
could not leave the dying man. Nor did Ethel wish him to do
so. Under these circumstances began the second beautiful
phase of Ethel's wooing, a sweet, daily correspondence, the
best of all preparations for matrimonial oneness and
understanding. Looking for Tyrrel's letters, reading them,
and answering them passed many happy hours, for to both it
was an absolute necessity to assure each other constantly,

"Since I wrote thee yester eve
I do love thee, Love, believe,
Twelve times dearer, twelve hours longer,
One dream deeper one night stronger,
One sun surer—this much more
Than I loved thee, dear, before."

And for the rest, she took up her old life with a fresh
enthusiasm.

Among these interests none were more urgent in their claims
than Dora Stanhope; and fortified by her grandmother's
opinion, Ethel went at once to call on her. She found Basil
with his wife, and his efforts to make Ethel see how much he

expected from her influence, and yet at the same time not even hint a disapproval of Dora, were almost pathetic, for he was so void of sophistry that his innuendoes were flagrantly open to detection. Dora felt a contempt for them, and he had hardly left the room ere she said:

"Basil has gone to his vestry in high spirits. When I told him you were coming to see me to-day he smiled like an angel. He believes you will keep me out of mischief, and he feels a grand confidence in something which he calls 'your influence.'"

"What do you mean by mischief?"

"Oh, I suppose going about with Fred Mostyn. I can't help that. I must have some one to look after me. All the young men I used to know pass me now with a lifted hat or a word or two. The girls have forgotten me. I don't suppose I shall be asked to a single dance this winter."

"The ladies in St. Jude's church would make a pet of you if—"

"The old cats and kittens! No, thank you, I am not going to church except on Sunday mornings—that is respectable and right; but as to being the pet of St. Jude's ladies! No, no! How they would mew over my delinquencies, and what scratches I should get from their velvet-shod claws! If I have to be talked about, I prefer the ladies of the world to discuss my frailties."

"But if I were you, I would give no one a reason for saying a word against me. Why should you?"

"Fred will supply them with reasons. I can't keep the man away from me. I don't believe I want to—he is very nice and useful."

"You are talking nonsense, things you don't mean, Dora. You are not such a foolish woman as to like to be seen with Fred Mostyn, that little monocular snob, after the aristocratic, handsome Basil Stanhope. The comparison is a mockery. Basil is the finest gentleman I ever saw. Socially, he is perfection, and—"

"He is only a clergyman."

"Even as a clergyman he is of religiously royal descent. There are generations of clergymen behind him, and he is a prince in the pulpit. Every man that knows him gives him the highest respect, every woman thinks you the most fortunate of wives. No one cares for Fred Mostyn. Even in his native place he is held in contempt. He had nine hundred votes to young Rawdon's twelve thousand."

"I don't mind that. I am going to the matinee to-morrow with Fred. He wanted to take me out in his auto this afternoon, but when I said I would go if you would he drew back. What is the reason? Did he make you offer of his hand? Did you refuse it?"

"He never made me an offer. I count that to myself as a great compliment. If he had done such a thing, he would certainly have been refused."

"I can tell that he really hates you. What dirty trick did you serve him about Rawdon Court?"

"So he called the release of Squire Rawdon a 'dirty trick'? It would have been a very dirty trick to have let Fred Mostyn get his way with Squire Rawdon."

"Of course, Ethel, when a man lends his money as an obligation he expects to get it back again."

"Mostyn got every farthing due him, and he wanted one of the finest manors in England in return for the obligation. He did not get it, thank God and my father!"

"He will not forget your father's interference."

"I hope he will remember it."

"Do you know who furnished the money to pay Fred? He says he is sure your father did not have it."

"Tell him to ask my father. He might even ask your father. Whether my father had the money or not was immaterial. Father could borrow any sum he wanted, I think."

"Whom did he borrow from?"

"I am sure that Fred told you to ask that question. Is he writing to you, Dora?"

"Suppose he is?"

"I cannot suppose such a thing. It is too impossible."

This was the beginning of a series of events all more or less qualified to bring about unspeakable misery in Basil's home. But there is nothing in life like the marriage tie. The tugs it will bear and not break, the wrongs it will look over, the chronic misunderstandings it will forgive, make it one of the mysteries of humanity. It was not in a day or a week that Basil Stanhope's dream of love and home was shattered. Dora had frequent and then less frequent times of return to her better self; and every such time renewed her husband's hope that she was merely passing through a period of transition and assimilation, and that in the end she would be all his desire hoped for.

Amelia E. Barr

But Ethel saw what he did not see, that Mostyn was gradually inspiring her with his own opinions, perhaps even with his own passion. In this emergency, however, she was gratified to find that Dora's mother appeared to have grasped the situation. For if Dora went to the theater with Mostyn, Mrs. Denning or Bryce was also there; and the reckless auto driving, shopping, and lunching had at least a show of respectable association. Yet when the opera season opened, the constant companionship of Mostyn and Dora became entirely too remarkable, not only in the public estimation, but in Basil's miserable conception of his own wrong. The young husband used every art and persuasion—and failed. And his failure was too apparent to be slighted. He became feverish and nervous, and his friends read his misery in eyes heavy with unshed tears, and in the wasting pallor caused by his sleepless, sorrowful nights.

Dora also showed signs of the change so rapidly working on her. She was sullen and passionate by turns; she complained bitterly to Ethel that her youth and beauty had been wasted; that she was only nineteen, and her life was over. She wanted to go to Paris, to get away from New York anywhere and anyhow. She began to dislike even the presence of Basil. His stately beauty offended her, his low, calm voice was the very keynote of irritation.

One morning near Christmas he came to her with a smiling, radiant face. "Dora," he said, "Dora, my love, I have something so interesting to tell you. Mrs. Colby and Mrs. Schaffler and some other ladies have a beautiful idea. They wish to give all the children of the church under eight years old the grandest Christmas tree imaginable—really rich presents and they thought you might like to have it here."

"What do you say, Basil!"

"You were always so fond of children. You—"

"I never could endure them."

"We all thought you might enjoy it. Indeed, I was so sure that I promised for you. It will be such a pleasure to me also, dear."

"I will have no such childish nonsense in my house."

"I promised it, Dora."

"You had no right to do so. This is my house. My father bought it and gave me it, and it is my own. I—"

"It seems, then, that I intrude in your house. Is it so? Speak, Dora."

"If you will ask questions you must take the answer. You do intrude when you come with such ridiculous proposals—in fact, you intrude very often lately."

"Does Mr. Mostyn intrude?"

"Mr. Mostyn takes me out, gives me a little sensible pleasure. You think I can be interested in a Christmas tree. The idea!"

"Alas, alas, Dora, you are tired of me! You do not love me! You do not love me!"

"I love nobody. I am sorry I got married. It was all a mistake. I will go home and then you can get a divorce."

At this last word the whole man changed. He was suffused, transfigured with an anger that was at once righteous and impetuous.

"How dare you use that word to me?" he demanded. "To the priest of God no such word exists. I do not know it. You are my wife, willing or unwilling. You are my wife forever, whether you dwell with me or not. You cannot sever bonds the Almighty has tied. You are mine, Dora Stanhope! Mine for time and eternity! Mine forever and ever!"

She looked at him in amazement, and saw a man after an image she had never imagined. She was terrified. She flung herself on the sofa in a whirlwind of passion. She cried aloud against his claim. She gave herself up to a vehement rage that was strongly infused with a childish dismay and panic.

"I will not be your wife forever!" she shrieked. "I will never be your wife again—never, not for one hour! Let me go! Take your hands off me!" For Basil had knelt down by the distraught woman, and clasping her in his arms said, even on her lips, "You ARE my dear wife! You are my very own dear wife! Tell me what to do. Anything that is right, reasonable I will do. We can never part."

"I will go to my father. I will never come back to you." And with these words she rose, threw off his embrace, and with a sobbing cry ran, like a terrified child, out of the room.

He sat down exhausted by his emotion, and sick with the thought she had evoked in that one evil word. The publicity, the disgrace, the wrong to Holy Church—ah, that was the cruelest wound! His own wrong was hard enough, but that he, who would gladly die for the Church, should put her to open shame! How could he bear it? Though it killed him, he must prevent that wrong; yes, if the right eye offended it must be plucked out. He must throw off his cassock, and turn away from the sacred aisles; he must—he could not say the word; he would wait a little. Dora would not leave him; it was impossible. He waited in a trance of aching suspense. Nothing for an hour or more broke it—no footfall, no sound of command or complaint. He was finally in hopes that Dora slept. Then he was called to lunch, and he made a pretense of eating it alone. Dora sent no excuse for her absence, and he could not trust himself to make inquiry about her. In the middle of the afternoon he heard a carriage drive to the door, and Dora, with her jewel-case in her hand, entered it and was driven away. The sight astounded him. He ran to her room, and found her maid packing her clothing. The woman answered his questions sullenly. She said "Mrs. Stanhope had gone to Mrs. Denning's, and had left orders for her trunks to be sent there." Beyond this she was silent and ignorant. No sympathy for either husband or wife was in her heart. Their quarrel was interfering with her own plans; she hated both of them in consequence.

In the meantime Dora had reached her home. Her mother was dismayed and hesitating, and her attitude raised again in Dora's heart the passion which had provoked the step she had taken. She wept like a lost child. She exclaimed against the horror of being Basil's wife forever and ever. She reproached her mother for suffering her to marry while she was only a child. She said she had been cruelly used in order to get the family into social recognition. She was in a frenzy of grief at her supposed sacrifice when her father came home. Her case was then won. With her arms round his neck, sobbing against his heart, her tears and entreaties on his lips, Ben Denning had no feeling and no care for anyone but his daughter. He took her view of things at once. "She HAD been badly used. It WAS a shame to tie a girl like Dora to sermons and such like. It was like shutting her up in a convent." Dora's tears and complaints fired him beyond reason. He promised her freedom whatever it cost him.

And while he sat in his private room considering the case, all the racial passions of his rough ancestry burning within him, Basil Stanhope called to see him. He permitted him to come into his presence, but he rose as he entered, and walked hastily a few steps to meet him.

"What do you want here, sir?" he asked.

"My wife."

"My daughter. You shall not see her. I have taken her back to my own care."

"She is my wife. No one can take her from me."

"I will teach you a different lesson."

"The law of God."

"The law of the land goes here. You'll find it more than you can defy."

"Sir, I entreat you to let me speak to Dora."

"I will not."

"I will stay here until I see her."

"I will give you five minutes. I do not wish to offer your profession an insult; if you have any respect for it you will obey me."

Answer me one question—what have I done wrong?"

"A man can be so intolerably right, that he becomes unbearably wrong. You have no business with a wife and a home. You are a d—sight too good for a good little girl that wants a bit of innocent amusement. Sermons and Christmas trees! Great Scott, what sensible woman would not be sick of it all? Sir, I don't want another minute of your company. Little wonder that my Dora is ill with it. Oblige me by leaving my house as quietly as possible." And he walked to the door, flung it open, and stood glaring at the distracted husband. "Go," he said. "Go at once. My lawyer will see you in the future. I have nothing further to say to you."

Basil went, but not to his desolate home. He had a private key to the vestry in his church, and in its darkness and solitude he faced the first shock of his ruined life, for he knew well all was over. All had been. He sank to the floor at the foot of the large cross which hung on its bare white walls. Grief's illimitable wave went over him, and like a drowning man he uttered an inarticulate cry of agony—the cry of a soul that had wronged its destiny. Love had betrayed him to ruin. All he had done must be abandoned. All he had won must be given up. Sin and shame indeed it would be if in his person a sacrament of the Church should be dragged through a divorce court. All other considerations paled before this disgrace. He must resign his curacy, strip himself of the honorable livery of heaven, obliterate his person and his name. It was a kind of death.

After awhile he rose, drank some water, lifted the shade and let the moonlight in. Then about that little room he walked with God through the long night, telling Him his sorrow and perplexity. And there is a depth in our own nature where the divine and human are one. That night Basil Stanhope found it, and henceforward knew that the bitterness of death was behind him, not before. "I made my nest too dear on earth," he sighed, "and it has been swept bare—that is, that I may build in heaven.

Amelia E. Barr

Now, the revelation of sorrow is the clearest of all revelations. Stanhope understood that hour what he must do. No doubts weakened his course. He went back to the house Dora called "hers," took away what he valued, and while the servants were eating their breakfast and talking over his marital troubles, he passed across its threshold for the last time. He told no one where he was going; he dropped as silently and dumbly out of the life that had known him as a stone dropped into mid-ocean.

Ethel considered herself fortunate in being from home at the time this disastrous culmination of Basil Stanhope's married life was reached. On that same morning the Judge, accompanied by Ruth and herself, had gone to Lenox to spend the holidays with some old friends, and she was quite ignorant of the matter when she returned after the New Year. Bryce was her first informant. He called specially to give her the news. He said his sister had been too ill and too busy to write. He had no word of sympathy for the unhappy pair. He spoke only of the anxiety it had caused him. "He was now engaged," he said, "to Miss Caldwell, and she was such an extremely proper, innocent lady, and a member of St. Jude's, it had really been a trying time for her." Bryce also reminded Ethel that he had been against Basil Stanhope from the first. "He had always known how that marriage would end," and so on.

Ethel declined to give any opinion. "She must hear both sides," she said. "Dora had been so reasonable lately, she had appeared happy."

"Oh, Dora is a little fox," he replied; "she doubles on herself always."

Ruth was properly regretful. She wondered "if any married woman was really happy." She did not apparently concern herself about Basil. The Judge rather leaned to Basil's consideration. He understood that Dora's overt act had shattered his professional career as well as his personal happiness. He could feel for the man there. "My dears," he said, with his dilettante air, "the goddess Calamity is delicate, and her feet are tender. She treads not upon the ground, but makes her path upon the hearts of men." In this non-committal way he gave his comment, for he usually found a bit of classical wisdom to fit modern emergencies, and the habit had imparted an antique bon-ton to his conversation. Ethel could only wonder at the lack of real sympathy.

In the morning she went to see her grandmother. The old lady had "heard" all she wanted to hear about Dora and Basil Stanhope. If men would marry a fool because she was young and pretty, they must take the consequences. "And why should Stanhope have married at all?" she asked indignantly. "No man can serve God and a woman at the same time. He had to be a bad priest and a good husband, or a bad husband and a good priest. Basil Stanhope was honored, was doing good, and he must needs be happy also. He wanted too much, and lost everything. Serve him right."

"All can now find some fault in poor Basil Stanhope," said Ethel. "Bryce was bitter against him because Miss Caldwell shivers at the word 'divorce.'"

"What has Bryce to do with Jane Caldwell?"

"He is going to marry her, he says."

"Like enough; she's a merry miss of two-score, and rich. Bryce's marriage with anyone will be a well-considered affair—a marriage with all the advantages of a good bargain. I'm tired of the whole subject. If women will marry they should be as patient as Griselda, in case there ever was such a woman; if not, there's an end of the matter."

"There are no Griseldas in this century, grandmother."

"Then there ought to be no marriages. Basil Stanhope was a grand man in public. What kind of a man was he in his home? Measure a man by his home conduct, and you'll not go wrong. It's the right place to draw your picture of him, I can tell you that."

"He has no home now, poor fellow."

"Whose fault was it? God only knows. Where is his wife?"

"She has gone to Paris."

"She has gone to the right place if she wants to play the fool. But there, now, God forbid I should judge her in the dark. Women should stand by women—considering."

"Considering?"

"What they may have to put up with. It is easy to see faults in others. I have sometimes met with people who should see faults in themselves. They are rather uncommon, though."

"I am sure Basil Stanhope will be miserable all his life. He will break his heart, I do believe."

"Not so. A good heart is hard to break, it grows strong in trouble. Basil Stanhope's body will fail long before his heart does; and even so an end must come to life, and after that peace or what God wills."

This scant sympathy Ethel found to be the usual tone among her acquaintances. St. Jude's got a new rector and a new idol, and the Stanhope affair was relegated to the limbo of things "it was proper to forget."

So the weeks of the long winter went by, and Ethel in the joy and hope of her own love-life naturally put out of her mind the sorrow of lives she could no longer help or influence. Indeed, as to Dora, there were frequent reports of her marvelous social success in Paris; and Ethel did not doubt Stanhope had found some everlasting gospel of holy work to comfort his desolation. And then also

> "Each day brings its petty dust,
> Our soon-choked souls to fill;
> And we forget because we must,
> And not because we will."

One evening when May with heavy clouds and slant rains was making the city as miserable as possible, Ethel had a caller. His card bore a name quite unknown, and his appearance gave no clew to his identity.

"Mr. Edmonds?" she said interrogatively.

"Are you Miss Ethel Rawdon?" he asked.

"Yes."

"Mr. Basil Stanhope told me to put this parcel in your hands."

"Oh, Mr. Stanhope! I am glad to hear from him. Where is he now?"

"We buried him yesterday. He died last Sunday as the bells were ringing for church—pneumonia, miss. While reading the service over a poor young man he had nursed many weeks he took cold. The poor will miss him sorely."

"DEAD!" She looked aghast at the speaker, and again ejaculated the pitiful, astounding word.

"Good evening, miss. I promised him to return at once to the work he left me to do." And he quietly departed, leaving Ethel standing with the parcel in her hands. She ran upstairs and locked it away. Just then she could not bear to open it.

"And it is hardly twelve months since he was married," she sobbed. "Oh, Ruth, Ruth, it is too cruel!"

"Dear," answered Ruth, "there is no death to such a man as Basil Stanhope."

"He was so young, Ruth."

"I know. 'His high-born brothers called him hence' at the age of twenty-nine, but

"'It is not growing like a tree,
In bulk, doth make men better be;
Or standing like an oak three hundred year,
To fall at last, dry, bald and sear:
A lily of a day
Is fairer far in May;
Although it fall and die that night,
It was the plant and flower of light.'"

At these words the Judge put down his Review to listen to Ethel's story, and when she ceased speaking he had gone far further back than any antique classic for compensation and satisfaction:

"He being made perfect in a short time fulfilled a long time.

For his soul pleased the Lord, therefore hasted He to take him away from among the wicked."[2] And that evening there was little conversation. Every heart was busy with its own thoughts.

[2] Wisdom of Solomon, IV., 13, 14.

CHAPTER XI

TRADE and commerce have their heroes as well as arms, and the struggle in which Tyrrel Rawdon at last plucked victory from apparent failure was as arduous a campaign as any military operations could have afforded. It had entailed on him a ceaseless, undaunted watch over antagonists rich and powerful; and a fight for rights which contained not only his own fortune, but the honor of his father, so that to give up a fraction of them was to turn traitor to the memory of a parent whom he believed to be beyond all doubt or reproach. Money, political power, civic influence, treachery, bribery, the law's delay and many other hindrances met him on every side, but his heart was encouraged daily to perseverance by love's tenderest sympathy. For he told Ethel everything, and received both from her fine intuitions and her father's legal skill priceless comfort and advice. But at last the long trial was over, the marriage day was set, and Tyrrel, with all his rights conceded, was honorably free to seek the happiness he had safeguarded on every side.

It was a lovely day in the beginning of May, nearly two years after their first meeting, when Tyrrel reached New York. Ethel knew at what hour his train would arrive, she was watching and listening for his step. They met in each other's arms, and the blessed hours of that happy evening were an over-payment of delight for the long months of their separation.

In the morning Ethel was to introduce her lover to Madam Rawdon, and side by side, almost hand in hand, they walked down the avenue together. Walked? They were so happy they hardly knew whether their feet touched earth or not. They had a constant inclination to clasp hands, to run as little children run; They wished to smile at everyone, to bid all the world good morning. Madam had resolved to be cool and careful in her advances, but she quickly found herself unable to resist the sight of so much love and hope and happiness. The young people together took her heart by storm, and she felt herself compelled to express an interest in their future, and to question Tyrrel about it.

"What are you going to do with yourself or make of yourself?" she asked Tyrrel one evening when they were sitting together. "I do hope you'll find some kind of work. Anything is better than loafing about clubs and such like places."

"I am going to study law with Judge Rawdon. My late experience has taught me its value. I do not think I shall loaf in his office."

"Not if he is anywhere around. He works and makes others work. Lawyering is a queer business, but men can be honest in it if they want to."

"And, grandmother," said Ethel, "my father says Tyrrel has a wonderful gift for public speaking. He made a fine speech at father's club last night. Tyrrel will go into politics."

"Will he, indeed? Tyrrel is a wonder. If he manages to walk his shoes straight in the zigzaggery ways of the law, he will be one of that grand breed called 'exceptions.' As for politics, I don't like them, far from it. Your grandfather used to say they either found a man a rascal or made him one. However,

I'm ready to compromise on law and politics. I was afraid with his grand voice he would set up for a tenor."

Tyrrel laughed. "I did once think of that role," he said.

"I fancied that. Whoever taught you to use your voice knew a thing or two about singing. I'll say that much."

"My mother taught me."

"Never! I wonder now!"

"She was a famous singer. She was a great and a good woman. I owe her for every excellent quality there is in me."

"No, you don't. You have got your black eyes and hair her way, I'll warrant that, but your solid make-up, your pluck and grit and perseverance is the Rawdon in you. Without Rawdon you would very likely now be strutting about some opera stage, playing at kings and lovemaking."

"As it is—"

"As it is, you will be lord consort of Rawdon Manor, with a silver mine to back you."

"I am sorry about the Manor," said Tyrrel. "I wish the dear old Squire were alive to meet Ethel and myself."

"To be sure you do. But I dare say that he is glad now to have passed out of it. Death is a mystery to those left, but I have no doubt it is satisfying to those who have gone away. He died as he lived, very properly; walked in the garden that morning as far as the strawberry beds, and the gardener gave him the first ripe half-dozen in a young cabbage leaf, and he ate them like a boy, and said they tasted as if grown in Paradise, then strolled home and asked Joel to shake the pillows on the sofa in the hall, laid himself down, shuffled his head easy among them, and fell on sleep. So Death the Deliverer found him. A good going home! Nothing to fear in it."

"Ethel tells me that Mr. Mostyn is now living at Mostyn Hall."

"Yes, he married that girl he would have sold his soul for and took her there, four months only after her husband's death. When I was young he durst not have done it, the Yorkshire gentry would have cut them both."

"I think," said Tyrrel, "American gentlemen of to-day felt much the same. Will Madison told me that the club cut him as soon as Mrs. Stanhope left her husband. He went there one day after it was known, and no one saw him; finally he walked up to McLean, and would have sat down, but McLean said, 'Your company is not desired, Mr. Mostyn.' Mostyn said something in reply, and McLean answered sternly, 'True, we are none of us saints, but there are lines the worst of us will not pass; and if there is any member of this club willing to interfere between a bridegroom and his bride, I would like to kick him out of it.' Mostyn struck the table with some exclamation, and McLean continued, 'Especially when the wronged husband is a gentleman of such stainless character and unsuspecting nature as Basil Stanhope—a clergyman also! Oh, the thing is beyond palliation entirely!' And he walked away and left Mostyn."

"Well," said Madam, "if it came to kicking, two could play that game. Fred is no coward. I don't want to hear another word about them. They will punish each other without our help. Let them alone. I hope you are not going to have a crowd at your wedding. The quietest weddings are the luckiest ones."

"About twenty of our most intimate friends are invited to the church," said Ethel. "There will be no reception until we return to New York in the fall."

"No need of fuss here, there will be enough when you reach Monk-Rawdon. The village will be garlanded and flagged, the bells ringing, and all your tenants and retainers out to meet you."

"We intend to get into our own home without anyone being aware of it. Come, Tyrrel, my dressmaker is waiting, I know. It is my wedding gown, dear Granny, and oh, so lovely!"

"You will not be any smarter than I intend to be, miss. You are shut off from color. I can outdo you."

"I am sure you can—and will. Here comes father. What can he want?" They met him at the door, and with a few laughing words left him with Madam. She looked curiously into his face and asked, "What is it, Edward?"

"I suppose they have told you all the arrangements. They are very simple. Did they say anything about Ruth?"

"They never named her. They said they were going to Washington for a week, and then to Rawdon Court. Ruth seems out of it all. Are you going to turn her adrift, or present her with a few thousand dollars? She has been a mother to Ethel. Something ought to be done for Ruth Bayard."

"I intend to marry her."

"I thought so."

"She will go to her sister's in Philadelphia for a month 's

preparation. I shall marry her there, and bring her home as my wife. She is a sweet, gentle, docile woman. She will make me happy."

"Sweet, gentle, docile! Yes, that is the style of wife Rawdon men prefer. What does Ethel say?"

"She is delighted. It was her idea. I was much pleased with her thoughtfulness. Any serious break in my life would now be a great discomfort. You need not look so satirical, mother; I thought of Ruth's life also."

"Also an afterthought; but Ruth is gentle and docile, and she is satisfied, and I am satisfied, so then everything is proper and everyone content. Come for me at ten on Wednesday morning. I shall be ready. No refreshments, I suppose. I must look after my own breakfast. Won't you feel a bit shabby, Edward? "And then the look and handclasp between them turned every word into sweetness and good-will.

And as Ethel regarded her marriage rather as a religious rite than a social function, she objected to its details becoming in any sense public, and her desires were to be regarded. Yet everyone may imagine the white loveliness of the bride, the joy of the bridegroom, the calm happiness of the family breakfast, and the leisurely, quiet leave-taking. The whole ceremony was the right note struck at the beginning of a new life, and they might justly expect it would move onward in melodious sequence.

Within three weeks after their marriage they arrived at Rawdon Court. It was on a day and at an hour when no one was looking for them, and they stepped into the lovely home waiting for them without outside observation. Hiring a carriage at the railway station, they dismissed it at the little bridge near the Manor House, and sauntered happily through

Amelia E. Barr

the intervening space. The door of the great hall stood open, and the fire, which had been burning on its big hearth unquenched for more than three hundred years, was blazing merrily, as if some hand had just replenished it. On the long table the broad, white beaver hat of the dead Squire was lying, and his oak walking stick was beside it. No one had liked to remove them. They remained just as he had put them down, that last, peaceful morning of his life.

In a few minutes the whole household was aware of their home-coming, and before the day was over the whole neighborhood. Then there was no way of avoiding the calls, the congratulations, and the entertainments that followed, and the old Court was once more the center of a splendid hospitality. Of course the Tyrrel-Rawdons were first on the scene, and Ethel was genuinely glad to meet again the good-natured Mrs. Nicholas. No one could give her better local advice, and Ethel quickly discovered that the best general social laws require a local interpretation. Her hands were full, her heart full, she had so many interests to share, so many people to receive and to visit, and yet when two weeks passed and Dora neither came nor wrote she was worried and dissatisfied.

"Are the Mostyns at the Hall?" she asked Mrs. Nicholas at last. "I have been expecting Mrs. Mostyn every day, but she neither comes nor writes to me."

"I dare say not. Poor little woman! I'll warrant she has been forbid to do either. If Mostyn thought she wanted to see you, he would watch day and night to prevent her coming. He's turning out as cruel a man as his father was, and you need not say a word worse than that."

"Cruel! Oh, dear, how dreadful! Men will drink and cheat and swear, but a cruel man seems so unnatural, so wicked."

"To be sure, cruelty is the joy of devils. As I said to John Thomas when we heard about Mostyn's goings-on, we have got rid of the Wicked One, but the wicked still remain with us."

This conversation having been opened, was naturally prolonged by the relation of incidents which had come through various sources to Mrs. Rawdon's ears, all of them indicating an almost incredible system of petty tyranny and cruel contradiction. Ethel was amazed, and finally angry at what she heard. Dora was her countrywoman and her friend; she instantly began to express her sympathy and her intention of interfering.

"You had better neither meddle nor make in the matter," answered Mrs. Rawdon. "Our Lucy went to see her, and gave her some advice about managing Yorkshiremen. And as she was talking Mostyn came in, and was as rude as he dared to be. Then Lucy asked him 'if he was sick.' She said, 'All the men in the neighborhood, gentle and simple, were talking about him, and that it wasn't a pleasant thing to be talked about in the way they were doing it. You must begin to look more like yourself, Mr. Mostyn; it is good advice I am giving you,' she added; and Mostyn told her he would look as he felt, whether it was liked or not liked. And Lucy laughed, and said, 'In that case he would have to go to his looking-glass for company.' Well, Ethel, there was a time to joy a devil after Lucy left, and some one of the servants went on their own responsibility for a doctor; and Mostyn ordered him out of the house, and he would not go until he saw Mrs. Mostyn; and the little woman was forced to come and say 'she was quite well,' though she was sobbing all the time she spoke. Then the doctor told Mostyn what he thought, and there is a quarrel between them every time they meet."

But Ethel was not deterred by these statements; on the

contrary, they stimulated her interest in her friend. Dora needed her, and the old feeling of protection stirred her to interference. At any rate, she could call and see the unhappy woman; and though Tyrrel was opposed to the visit, and thought it every way unwise, Ethel was resolved to make it. "You can drive me there," she said, "then go and see Justice Manningham and call for me in half an hour." And this resolution was strengthened by a pitiful little note received from Dora just after her decision. "Mostyn has gone to Thirsk," it said; "for pity's sake come and see me about two o'clock this afternoon."

The request was promptly answered. As the clock struck two Ethel crossed the threshold of the home that might have been hers. She shuddered at the thought. The atmosphere of the house was full of fear and gloom, the furniture dark and shabby, and she fancied the wraiths of old forgotten crimes and sorrows were gliding about the sad, dim rooms and stairways. Dora rose in a passion of tears to welcome her, and because time was short instantly began her pitiful story.

"You know how he adored me once," she said; "would you believe it, Ethel, we were not two weeks married when he began to hate me. He dragged me through Europe in blazing heat and blinding snows when I was sick and unfit to move. He brought me here in the depth of winter, and when no one called on us he blamed me; and from morning till night, and sometimes all night long, he taunts and torments me. After he heard that you had bought the Manor he lost all control of himself. He will not let me sleep. He walks the floor hour after hour, declaring he could have had you and the finest manor in England but for a cat-faced woman like me. And he blames me for poor Basil's death—says we murdered him together, and that he sees blood on my hands." And she looked with terror at her small, thin hands, and held them up as if to protest against the charge. When she next spoke it was to sob out, "Poor Basil! He would pity me! He would help me! He would forgive me! He knows now that Mostyn was, and is, my evil genius."

"Do not cry so bitterly, Dora, it hurts me. Let us think. Is there nothing you can do?"

"I want to go to mother." Then she drew Ethel's head close to her and whispered a few words, and Ethel answered, "You poor little one, you shall go to your mother. Where is she?"

"She will be in London next week, and I must see her. He will not let me go, but go I must if I die for it. Mrs. John Thomas Rawdon told me what to do, and I have been following her advice."

Ethel did not ask what it was, but added,

"If Tyrrel and I can help you, send for us. We will come. And, Dora, do stop weeping, and be brave. Remember you are an American woman. Your father has often told me how you could ride with Indians or cowboys and shoot with any miner in Colorado. A bully like Mostyn is always a coward. Lift up your heart and stand for every one of your rights. You will find plenty of friends to stand with you." And with the words she took her by the hands and raised her to her feet, and looked at her with such a beaming, courageous smile that Dora caught its spirit, and promised to insist on her claims for rest and sleep.

"When shall I come again, Dora?"

"Not till I send for you. Mother will be in London next Wednesday at the Savoy. I intend to leave here Wednesday some time, and may need you; will you come?"

Amelia E. Barr

"Surely, both Tyrrel and I."

Then the time being on a dangerous line they parted. But Ethel could think of nothing and talk of nothing but the frightful change in her friend, and the unceasing misery which had produced it. Tyrrel shared all her indignation. The slow torture of any creature was an intolerable crime in his eyes, but when the brutality was exercised on a woman, and on a country-woman, he was roused to the highest pitch of indignation. When Wednesday arrived he did not leave the house, but waited with Ethel for the message they confidently expected. It came about five o'clock—urgent, imperative, entreating, "Come, for God's sake! He will kill me."

The carriage was ready, and in half an hour they were at Mostyn Hall. No one answered their summons, but as they stood listening and waiting, a shrill cry of pain and anger pierced the silence. It was followed by loud voices and a confused noise—noise of many talking and exclaiming. Then Tyrrel no longer hesitated. He opened the door easily, and taking Ethel on his arm, suddenly entered the parlor from which the clamor came. Dora stood in the center of the room like an enraged pythoness, her eyes blazing with passion.

"See!" she cried as Tyrrel entered the room—"see!" And she held out her arm, and pointed to her shoulder from which the lace hung in shreds, showing the white flesh, red and bruised, where Mostyn had gripped her. Then Tyrrel turned to Mostyn, who was held tightly in the grasp of his gardener and coachman, and foaming with a rage that rendered his explanation almost inarticulate, especially as the three women servants gathered around their mistress added their railing and invectives to the general confusion.

"The witch! The cat-faced woman!" he screamed. "She

wants to go to her mother! Wants to play the trick she killed Basil Stanhope with! She shall not! She shall not! I will kill her first! She is mad! I will send her to an asylum! She is a little devil! I will send her to hell! Nothing is bad enough—nothing—"

"Mr. Mostyn," said Tyrrel.

"Out of my house! What are you doing here? Away! This is my house! Out of it immediately!"

"This man is insane," said Tyrrel to Dora. "Put on your hat and cloak, and come home with us."

"I am waiting for Justice Manningham," she answered with a calm subsidence of passion that angered Mostyn more than her reproaches. "I have sent for him. He will be here in five minutes now. That brute"—pointing to Mostyn—"must be kept under guard till I reach my mother. The magistrate will bring a couple of constables with him."

"This is a plot, then! You hear it! You! You, Tyrrel Rawdon, and you, Saint Ethel, are in it, all here on time. A plot, I say! Let me loose that I may strangle the cat-faced creature. Look at her hands, they are already bloody!"

At these words Dora began to sob passionately, the servants, one and all, to comfort her, or to abuse Mostyn, and in the height of the hubbub Justice Manningham entered with two constables behind him.

"Take charge of Mr. Mostyn," he said to them, and as they laid their big hands on his shoulders the Justice added, "You will consider yourself under arrest, Mr. Mostyn."

And when nothing else could cow Mostyn, he was cowed by

Amelia E. Barr

the law. He sank almost fainting into his chair, and the Justice listened to Dora's story, and looked indignantly at the brutal man, when she showed him her torn dress and bruised shoulder. "I entreat your Honor," she said, "to permit me to go to my mother who is now in London." And he answered kindly, "You shall go. You are in a condition only a mother can help and comfort. As soon as I have taken your deposition you shall go."

No one paid any attention to Mostyn's disclaimers and denials. The Justice saw the state of affairs. Squire Rawdon and Mrs. Rawdon testified to Dora's ill-usage; the butler, the coachman, the stablemen, the cook, the housemaids were all eager to bear witness to the same; and Mrs. Mostyn's appearance was too eloquent a plea for any humane man to deny her the mother-help she asked for.

Though neighbors and members of the same hunt and clubs, the Justice took no more friendly notice of Mostyn than he would have taken of any wife-beating cotton-weaver; and when all lawful preliminaries had been arranged, he told Mrs. Mostyn that he should not take up Mr. Mostyn's case till Friday; and in the interval she would have time to put herself under her mother's care. She thanked him, weeping, and in her old, pretty way kissed his hands, and "vowed he had saved her life, and she would forever remember his goodness." Mostyn mocked at her "play-acting," and was sternly reproved by the Justice; and then Tyrrel and Ethel took charge of Mrs. Mostyn until she was ready to leave for London.

She was more nearly ready than they expected. All her trunks were packed, and the butler promised to take them immediately to the railway station. In a quarter of an hour she appeared in traveling costume, with her jewels in a bag, which she carried in her hand. There was a train for London passing Monk-Rawdon at eight o'clock; and after Justice Manningham had left, the cook brought in some dinner, which Dora asked the Rawdons to share with her. It was, perhaps, a necessary but a painful meal. No one noticed Mostyn. He was enforced to sit still and watch its progress, which he accompanied with curses it would be a kind of sacrilege to write down. But no one answered him, and no one noticed the orders he gave for his own dinner, until Dora rose to leave forever the house of bondage. Then she said to the cook:

"See that those gentlemanly constables have something good to eat and to drink, and when they have been served you may give that man"—pointing to Mostyn—"the dinner of bread and water he has so often prescribed for me. After my train leaves you are all free to go to your own homes. Farewell, friends!"

Then Mostyn raved again, and finally tried his old loving terms. "Come back to me, Dora," he called frantically. "Come back, dearest, sweetest Dora, I will be your lover forever. I will never say another cross word to you."

But Dora heard not and saw not. She left the room without a glance at the man sitting cowering between the officers, and blubbering with shame and passion and the sense of total loss. In a few minutes he heard the Rawdon carriage drive to the door. Tyrrel and Ethel assisted Dora into it, and the party drove at once to the railway station. They were just able to catch the London train. The butler came up to report all the trunks safely forwarded, and Dora dropped gold into his hand, and bade him clear the house of servants as soon as the morning broke. Fortunately there was no time for last words and promises; the train began to move, and Tyrrel and Ethel, after watching Dora's white face glide into the darkness, turned silently away. That depression which so often follows the lifting of burdens not intended for our shoulders weighed on their hearts and made speech difficult. Tyrrel was especially affected by it. A quick feeling of something like sympathy for Mostyn would not be reasoned away, and he drew Ethel close within his arm, and gave the coachman an order to drive home as quickly as possible, for twilight was already becoming night, and under the trees the darkness felt oppressive.

The little fire on the hearth and their belated dinner somewhat relieved the tension; but it was not until they had retired to a small parlor, and Tyrrel had smoked a cigar, that the tragedy of the evening became a possible topic of conversation. Tyrrel opened the subject by a question as to whether "he ought to have gone with Dora to London."

"Dora opposed the idea strongly when I named it to her," answered Ethel. "She said it would give opportunities for Mostyn to slander both herself and you, and I think she was correct. Every way she was best alone."

"Perhaps, but I feel as if I ought to have gone, as if I had been something less than a gentleman; in fact, as if I had been very ungentle."

"There is no need," answered Ethel a little coldly.

"It is a terrible position for Mostyn."

"He deserves it."

"He is so sensitive about public opinion."

"In that case he should behave decently in private."

Then Tyrrel lit another cigar, and there was another silence, which Ethel occupied in irritating thoughts of Dora's unfortunate fatality in trouble-making. She sat at a little table standing between herself and Tyrrel. It held his smoking utensils, and after awhile she pushed them aside, and let the splendid rings which adorned her hand fall into the cleared space. Tyrrel watched her a few moments, and then asked, "What are you doing, Ethel, my dear?"

She looked up with a smile, and then down at the hand she had laid open upon the table. "I am looking at the Ring of all Rings. See, Tyrrel, it is but a little band of gold, and yet it gave me more than all the gems of earth could buy. Rubies and opals and sapphires are only its guard. The simple wedding ring is the ring of great price. It is the loveliest ornament a happy woman can wear."

Tyrrel took her hand and kissed it, and kissed the golden band, and then answered, "Truly an ornament if a happy wife wears it; but oh, Ethel, what is it when it binds a woman to such misery as Dora has just fled from?"

"Then it is a fetter, and a woman who has a particle of self-respect will break it. The Ring of all Rings!" she ejaculated again, as she lifted the rubies and opals, and slowly but smilingly encircled the little gold band.

"Let us try now to forget that sorrowful woman," said Tyrrel. "She will be with her mother in a few hours. Mother-love can cure all griefs. It never fails. It never blames. It never grows weary. It is always young and warm and true. Dora will be comforted. Let us forget; we can do no more."

For a couple of days this was possible, but then came Mrs. Nicholas Rawdon, and the subject was perforce opened. "It was a bad case," she said, "but it is being settled as quickly and as quietly as possible. I believe the man has entered into some sort of recognizance to keep the peace, and has disappeared. No one will look for him. The gentry are against pulling one another down in any way, and this affair they don't want talked about. Being all of them married men, it isn't to be expected, is it? Justice Manningham was very sorry for the little lady, but he said also 'it was a bad precedent, and ought not to be discussed.' And Squire Bentley said, 'If English gentlemen would marry American women, they must put up with American women's ways,' and so on. None of them think it prudent to approve Mrs. Mostyn's course. But they won't get off as easy as they think. The women are standing up for her. Did you ever hear anything like that? And I'll warrant some husbands are none so easy in their minds, as my Nicholas said, 'Mrs. Mostyn had sown seed that would be seen and heard tell of for many a long day.' Our Lucy, I suspect, had more to do with the move than she will confess. She got a lot of new, queer notions at college, and I do believe in my heart she set the poor woman up to the business. John Thomas, of course, says not a word, but he looks at Lucy in a very proud kind of way; and I'll be bound he has got an object lesson he'll remember as long as he lives. So has Nicholas, though he bluffs more than a little as to what he'd do with a wife that got a running-away notion into her head. Bless you, dear, they are all formulating their laws on the subject, and their wives are smiling queerly at them, and holding their heads a bit higher than usual. I've been doing it myself, so I know how they feel."

Thus, though very little was said in the newspapers about the affair, the notoriety Mostyn dreaded was complete and thorough. It was the private topic of conversation in every household. Men talked it over in all the places where men met, and women hired the old Mostyn servants in order to get the very surest and latest story of the poor wife's wrongs, and then compared reports and even discussed the circumstances in their own particular clubs.

At the Court, Tyrrel and Ethel tried to forget, and their own interests were so many and so important that they usually succeeded; especially after a few lines from Mrs. Denning assured them of Dora's safety and comfort. And for many weeks the busy life of the Manor sufficed; there was the hay to cut in the meadow lands, and after it the wheat fields to harvest. The stables, the kennels, the farms and timber, the park and the garden kept Tyrrel constantly busy. And to these duties were added the social ones, the dining and dancing and entertaining, the horse racing, the regattas, and the enthusiasm which automobiling in its first fever engenders.

And yet there were times when Tyrrel looked bored, and when nothing but Squire Percival's organ or Ethel's piano seemed to exorcise the unrest and ennui that could not be hid. Ethel watched these moods with a wise and kind curiosity, and in the beginning of September, when they perceptibly increased, she asked one day, "Are you happy, Tyrrel? Quite happy?"

"I am having a splendid holiday," he answered, "but—"

"But what, dear?"

"One could not turn life into a long holiday—that would be harder than the hardest work."

She answered "Yes," and as soon as she was alone fell to thinking, and in the midst of her meditation Mrs. Nicholas Rawdon entered in a whirl of tempestuous delight.

"What do you think?" she asked between laughing and crying. "Whatever do you think? Our Lucy had twins

Amelia E. Barr

yesterday, two fine boys as ever was. And I wish you could see their grandfather and their father. They are out of themselves with joy. They stand hour after hour beside the two cradles, looking at the little fellows, and they nearly came to words this morning about their names."

"I am so delighted!" cried Ethel. "And what are you going to call them?"

"One is an hour older than the other, and John Thomas wanted them called Percival and Nicholas. But my Nicholas wanted the eldest called after himself, and he said so plain enough. And John Thomas said 'he could surely name his own sons; and then Nicholas told him to remember he wouldn't have been here to have any sons at all but for his father.' And just then I came into the room to have a look at the little lads, and when I heard what they were fratching about, I told them it was none of their business, that Lucy had the right to name the children, and they would just have to put up with the names she gave them."

"And has Lucy named them?"

"To be sure. I went right away to her and explained the dilemma, and I said, 'Now, Lucy, it is your place to settle this question.' And she answered in her positive little way, 'You tell father the eldest is to be called Nicholas, and tell John Thomas the youngest is to be called John Thomas. I can manage two of that name very well. And say that I won't have any more disputing about names, the boys are as good as christened already.' And of course when Lucy said that we all knew it was settled. And I'm glad the eldest is Nicholas. He is a fine, sturdy little York-shireman, bawling out already for what he wants, and flying into a temper if he doesn't get it as soon as he wants it. Dearie me, Ethel, I am a proud woman this morning. And Nicholas is going to give all the hands a holiday, and a trip up to Ambleside on Saturday, though John Thomas is very much against it."

"Why is he against it?"

"He says they will be holding a meeting on Monday night to try and find out what Old Nicholas is up to, and that if he doesn't give them the same treat on the same date next year, they'll hold an indignation meeting about being swindled out of their rights. And I'll pledge you my word John Thomas knows the men he's talking about. However, Nicholas is close with his money, and it will do him good happen to lose a bit. Blood-letting is healthy for the body, and perhaps gold-letting may help the soul more than we think for."

This news stimulated Ethel's thinking, and when she also stood beside the two cradles, and the little Nicholas opened his big blue eyes and began to "bawl for what he wanted," a certain idea took fast hold of her, and she nursed it silently for the next month, watching Tyrrel at the same time. It was near October, however, before she found the proper opportunity for speaking. There had been a long letter from the Judge. It said Ruth and he were home again after a wonderful trip over the Northern Pacific road. He wrote with enthusiasm of the country and its opportunities, and of the big cities they had visited on their return from the Pacific coast. Every word was alive, the magnitude and stir of traffic and wrestling humanity seemed to rustle the paper. He described New York as overflowing with business. His own plans, the plans of others, the jar of politics, the thrill of music and the drama—all the multitudinous vitality that crowded the streets and filled the air, even to the roofs of the twenty-story buildings, contributed to the potent exhilaration of the letter.

"Great George!" exclaimed Tyrrel. "That is life! That is

living! I wish we were back in America!"

"So do I, Tyrrel."

"I am so glad. When shall we go? It is now the twenty-eighth of September."

"Are you very weary of Rawdon Court'"

"Yes. If a man could live for the sake of eating and sleeping and having a pleasant time, why Rawdon Court would be a heaven to him; but if he wants to DO something with his life, he would be most unhappy here."

"And you want to do something?"

"You would not have loved a man who did not want TO DO. We have been here four months. Think of it! If I take four months out of every year for twenty years, I shall lose, with travel, about seven years of my life, and the other things to be dropped with them may be of incalculable value."

"I see, Tyrrel. I am not bound in any way to keep Rawdon Court. I can sell it tomorrow."

"But you would be grieved to do so?"

"Not at all. Being a lady of the Manor does not flatter me. The other squires would rather have a good man in my place."

"Why did you buy it?"

"As I have told you, to keep Mostyn out, and to keep a Rawdon here. But Nicholas Rawdon craves the place, and will pay well for his desire. It cost me eighty thousand pounds. He told father he would gladly give me one hundred thousand pounds whenever I was tired of my bargain. I will take the hundred thousand pounds to-morrow. There would then be four good heirs to Rawdon on the place."

Here the conversation was interrupted by Mrs. Nicholas, who came to invite them to the christening feast of the twins. Tyrrel soon left the ladies together, and Ethel at once opened the desired conversation.

"I am afraid we may have left the Court before the christening," she said. "Mr. Rawdon is very unhappy here. He is really homesick."

"But this is his home, isn't it? And a very fine one."

"He cannot feel it so. He has large interests in America. I doubt if I ever induce him to come here again. You see, this visit has been our marriage trip."

"And you won't live here! I never heard the line. What will you do with the Court? It will be badly used if it is left to servants seven or eight months every year."

"I suppose I must sell it. I see no—"

"If you only would let Nicholas buy it. You might be sure then it would be well cared for, and the little lads growing up in it, who would finally heir it. Oh, Ethel, if you would think of Nicholas first. He would honor the place and be an honor to it."

Out of this conversation the outcome was as satisfactory as it was certain, and within two weeks Nicholas Rawdon was Squire of Rawdon Manor, and possessor of the famous old Manor House. Then there followed a busy two weeks for

Tyrrel, who had the superintendence of the packing, which was no light business. For though Ethel would not denude the Court of its ancient furniture and ornaments, there were many things belonging to the personal estate of the late Squire which had been given to her by his will, and could not be left behind. But by the end of October cases and trunks were all sent off to the steamship in which their passage was taken; and the Rawdon estate, which had played such a momentous part in Ethel's life having finished its mission, had no further influence, and without regret passed out of her physical life forever.

Indeed, their willingness to resign all claims to the old home was a marvel to both Tyrrel and Ethel. On their last afternoon there they walked through the garden, and stood under the plane tree where their vows of love had been pledged, and smiled and wondered at their indifference. The beauteous glamor of first love was gone as completely as the flowers and scents and songs that had then filled the charming place. But amid the sweet decay of these things they once more clasped hands, looking with supreme confidence into each other's eyes. All that had then been promised was now certain; and with an affection infinitely sweeter and surer, Tyrrel drew Ethel to his heart, and on her lips kissed the tenderest, proudest words a woman hears, "My dear wife!"

This visit was their last adieu, all the rest had been said, and early the next morning they left Monk-Rawdon station as quietly as they had arrived. During their short reign at Rawdon Court they had been very popular, and perhaps their resignation was equally so. After all, they were foreigners, and Nicholas Rawdon was Yorkshire, root and branch.

"Nice young people," said Justice Manningham at a hunt dinner, "but our ways are not their ways, nor like to be. The young man was born a fighter, and there are neither bears nor Indians here for him to fight; and our politics are Greek to him; and the lady, very sweet and beautiful, but full of new ideas—ideas not suitable for women, and we do not wish our women changed."

"Good enough as they are," mumbled Squire Oakes.

"Nicest Americans I ever met," added Earl Danvers, "but Nicholas Rawdon will be better at Rawdon Court." To which statement there was a general assent, and then the subject was considered settled.

In the meantime Tyrrel and Ethel had reached London and gone to the Metropole Hotel; because, as Ethel said, no one knew where Dora was; but if in England, she was likely to be at the Savoy. They were to be two days in London. Tyrrel had banking and other business to fully occupy the time, and Ethel remembered she had some shopping to do, a thing any woman would discover if she found herself in the neighborhood of Regent Street and Piccadilly. On the afternoon of the second day this duty was finished, and she returned to her hotel satisfied but a little weary. As she was going up the steps she noticed a woman coming slowly down them. It was Dora Mostyn. They met with great enthusiasm on Dora's part, and she turned back and went with Ethel to her room.

Ethel looked at her with astonishment. She was not like any Dora she had previously seen. Her beauty had developed wondrously, she had grown much taller, and her childish manner had been superseded by a carriage and air of superb grace and dignity. She had now a fine color, and her eyes were darker, softer, and more dreamy than ever. "Take off your hat, Dora," said Ethel, "and tell me what has happened. You are positively splendid. Where is Mr. Mostyn?"

"I neither know nor care. He is tramping round the world after me, and I intend to keep him at it. But I forget. I must tell you how THAT has come about."

"We heard from Mrs. Denning. She said she had received you safely."

"My dear mother! She met me like an angel; comforted and cared for me, never said one word of blame, only kissed and pitied me. We talked things over, and she advised me to go to New York. So we took three passages under the names of Mrs. John Gifford, Miss Gifford, and Miss Diana Gifford. Miss Diana was my maid, but mother thought a party of three would throw Mostyn off our track."

"A very good idea."

"We sailed at once. On the second day out I had a son. The poor little fellow died in a few hours, and was buried at sea. But his birth has given me the power to repay to Fred Mostyn some of the misery he caused me."

"How so? I do not see."

"Oh, you must see, if you will only remember how crazy Englishmen are about their sons. Daughters don't count, you know, but a son carries the property in the family name. He is its representative for the next generation. As I lay suffering and weeping, a fine scheme of revenge came clearly to me. Listen! Soon after we got home mother cabled Mostyn's lawyer that 'Mrs. Mostyn had had a son.' Nothing was said of the boy's death. Almost immediately I was notified that Mr. Mostyn would insist on the surrender of the child to his care. I took no notice of the letters. Then he sent his lawyer to claim the child and a woman to take care of it. I laughed them to scorn, and defied them to find the child. After them came Mostyn himself. He interviewed doctors, overlooked baptismal registers, advertised far and wide, bribed our servants, bearded father in his office, abused Bryce on the avenue, waylaid me in all my usual resorts, and bombarded me with letters, but he knows no more yet than the cable told him. And the man is becoming a monomaniac about HIS SON."

"Are you doing right, Dora?"

"If you only knew how he had tortured me! Father and mother think he deserves all I can do to him. Anyway, he will have it to bear. If he goes to the asylum he threatened me with, I shall be barely satisfied. The 'cat-faced woman' is getting her innings now."

"Have you never spoken to him or written to him? Surely"

"He caught me one day as I came out of our house, and said, 'Madam, where is my son?' And I answered, 'You have no son. The child WAS MINE. You shall never see his face in this world. I have taken good care of that.'"

"'I will find him some day,' he said, and I laughed at him, and answered, 'He is too cunningly hid. Do you think I would let the boy know he had such a father as you? No, indeed. Not unless there was property for the disgrace.' I touched him on the raw in that remark, and then I got into my carriage and told the coachman to drive quickly. Mostyn attempted to follow me, but the whip lashing the horses was in the way." And Dora laughed, and the laugh was cruel and mocking and full of meaning.

"Dora, how can you? How can you find pleasure in such revenges,"

Amelia E. Barr

"I am having the greatest satisfaction of my life. And I am only beginning the just retribution, for my beauty is enthralling the man again, and he is on the road to a mad jealousy of me."

"Why don't you get a divorce? This is a case for that remedy. He might then marry again, and you also."

"Even so, I should still torment him. If he had sons he would be miserable in the thought that his unknown son might, on his death, take from them the precious Mostyn estate, and that wretched, old, haunted house of his. I am binding him to misery on every hand."

"Is Mrs. Denning here with you?"

"Both my father and mother are with me. Father is going to take a year's rest, and we shall visit Berlin, Vienna, Rome, Paris or wherever our fancy leads us."

"And Mr. Mostyn?"

"He can follow me round, and see nobles and princes and kings pay court to the beauty of the 'cat-faced woman.' I shall never notice him, never speak to him; but you need not look so suspicious, Ethel. Neither by word nor deed will I break a single convention of the strictest respectability."

"Mr. Mostyn ought to give you your freedom."

"I have given freedom to myself. I have already divorced him. When they brought my dead baby for me to kiss, I slipped into its little hand the ring that made me his mother. They went to the bottom of the sea together. As for ever marrying again, not in this life. I have had enough of it. My first husband was the sweetest saint out of heaven, and my second was some mean little demon that had sneaked his way out of hell; and I found both insupportable." She lifted her hat as she spoke, and began to pin it on her beautifully dressed hair. "Have no fear for me," she continued. "I am sure Basil watches over me. Some day I shall be good, and he will be happy." Then, hand in hand, they walked to the door together, and there were tears in both voices as they softly said "Good-by."

Amelia E. Barr

CHAPTER XII

A WEEK after this interview Tyrrel and Ethel were in New York. They landed early in the morning, but the Judge and Ruth were on the pier to meet them; and they breakfasted together at the fashionable hotel, where an elegant suite had been reserved for the residence of the Tyrrel-Rawdons until they had perfected their plans for the future. Tyrrel was boyishly excited, but Ethel's interest could not leave her father and his new wife. These two had lived in the same home for fifteen years, and then they had married each other, and both of them looked fifteen years younger. The Judge was actually merry, and Ruth, in spite of her supposed "docility," had quite reversed the situation. It was the Judge who was now docile, and even admiringly obedient to all Ruth's wifely advices and admonitions.

The breakfast was a talkative, tardy one, but at length the Judge went to his office and Tyrrel had to go to the Custom House. Ethel was eager to see her grandmother, and she was sure the dear old lady was anxiously waiting her arrival. And Ruth was just as anxious for Ethel to visit her renovated home. She had the young wife's delight in its beauty, and she wanted Ethel to admire it with her.

"We will dine with you to-morrow, Ruth," said Ethel, "and I will come very early and see all the improvements. I feel sure the house is lovely, and I am glad father made you such a pretty nest. Nothing is too pretty for you, Ruth." And there was no insincerity in this compliment. These two women knew and loved and trusted each other without a shadow of doubt or variableness.

So Ruth went to her home, and Ethel hastened to Gramercy Park. Madam was eagerly watching for her arrival.

"I have been impatient for a whole hour, all in a quiver, dearie," she cried. "It is nearly noon."

"I have been impatient also, Granny, but father and Ruth met us at the pier and stayed to breakfast with us, and you know how men talk and talk."

"Ruth and father down at the pier! How you dream!"

"They were really there. And they do seem so happy, grandmother. They are so much in love with each other."

"I dare say. There are no fools like old fools. So you have sold the Court to Nicholas Rawdon, and a cotton-spinner is Lord of the Manor. Well, well, how are the mighty fallen!"

"I made twenty thousand pounds by the sale. Nicholas Rawdon is a gentleman, and John Thomas is the most popular man in all the neighborhood. And, Granny, he has two sons—twins—the handsomest little chaps you ever saw. No fear of a Rawdon to heir the Manor now."

"Fortune is a baggage. When she is ill to a man she knows no reason. She sent John Thomas to Parliament, and kept Fred out at a loss, too. She took the Court from Fred and gave it to John Thomas, and she gives him two sons about the same time she gives Fred one, and that one she kidnaps out of his

Amelia E. Barr

sight and knowledge. Poor Fred!"

"Well, grandmother, it is 'poor Fred's' own doing, and, I assure you, Fred would have been most unwelcome at the Court. And the squires and gentry round did not like a woman in the place; they were at a loss what to do with me. I was no good for dinners and politics and hunting. I embarrassed them." "Of course you would. They would have to talk decently and behave politely, and they would not be able to tell their choicest stories. Your presence would be a bore; but could not Tyrrel take your place?"

"Granny, Tyrrel was really unhappy in that kind of life. And he was a foreigner, so was I. You know what Yorkshire people think of foreigners. They were very courteous, but they were glad to have the Yorkshire Rawdons in our place. And Tyrrel did not like working with the earth; he loves machinery and electricity."

"To be sure. When a man has got used to delving for gold or silver, cutting grass and wheat does seem a slow kind of business."

"And he disliked the shut-up feeling the park gave him. He said we were in the midst of solitude three miles thick. It made him depressed and lonely."

"That is nonsense. I am sure on the Western plains he had solitude sixty miles thick—often."

"Very likely, but then he had an horizon, even if it were sixty miles away. And no matter how far he rode, there was always that line where earth seemed to rise to heaven. But the park was surrounded by a brick wall fourteen feet high. It had no horizon. You felt as if you were in a large, green box—at least Tyrrel did. The wall was covered with roses and ivy, but still it was a boundary you could not pass, and could not see over. Don't you understand, Granny, how Tyrrel would feel this?"

"I can't say I do. Why didn't he come with you?"

"He had to go to the Customs about our trunks, and there were other things. He will see you to-morrow. Then we are going to dine with father, and if you will join us, we will call at six for you. Do, Granny."

"Very well, I shall be ready." But after a moment's thought she continued, "No, I will not go. I am only a mortal woman, and the company of angels bores me yet."

"Now, Granny, dear."

"I mean what I say. Your father has married such a piece of perfection that I feel my shortcomings in her presence more than I can bear. But I'll tell you what, dearie, Tyrrel may come for me Saturday night at six, and I will have my dinner with you. I want to see the dining-room of a swell hotel in full dress; and I will wear my violet satin and white Spanish lace, and look as smart as can be, dear. And Tyrrel may buy me a bunch of white violets. I am none too old to wear them. Who knows but I may go to the theater also?"

"Oh, Granny, you are just the dearest young lady I know! Tyrrel will be as proud as a peacock."

"Well, I am not as young as I might be, but I am a deal younger than I look. Listen, dearie, I have never FELT old yet! Isn't that a thing to be grateful for? I don't read much poetry, except it be in the Church Hymnal, but I cut a verse out of a magazine a year ago which just suits my idea of life, and, what is still more wonderful, I took the trouble to learn it. Oliver Wendell Holmes wrote it, and I'll warrant him for a good, cheerful, trust-in-God man, or he'd never have thought of such sensible words."

"I am listening, Granny, for the verse."

"Yes, and learn it yourself. It will come in handy some day, when Tyrrel and you are getting white-haired and handsome, as everyone ought to get when they have passed their half-century and are facing the light of the heavenly world:

> "At sixty-two life has begun;
> At seventy-three begins once more;
> Fly swifter as thou near'st the sun,
> And brighter shine at eighty-four.
> At ninety-five,
> Should thou arrive,
> Still wait on God, and work and thrive."

Such words as those, Ethel, keep a woman young, and make her right glad that she was born and thankful that she lives."

"Thank you for them, dear Granny. Now I must run away as fast as I can. Tyrrel will be wondering what has happened to me."

In this conjecture she was right. Tyrrel was in evening dress, and walking restlessly about their private parlor. "Ethel," he said, plaintively, "I have been so uneasy about you."

"I am all right, dearest. I was with grandmother. I shall be ready in half an hour."

Even if she had been longer, she would have earned the delay, for she returned to him in pink silk and old Venice point de rose, with a pretty ermine tippet across her shoulders. It was a joy to see her, a delight to hear her speak, and she walked as if she heard music. The dining-room was crowded when they entered, but they made a sensation. Many rose and came to welcome them home. Others smiled across the busy space and lifted their wineglass in recognition. The room was electric, sensitive and excited. It was flooded with a soft light; it was full of the perfume of flowers. The brilliant coloring of silks and satins, and the soft miracle of white lace blended with the artistically painted walls and roof. The aroma of delicate food, the tinkle of crystal, the low murmur of happy voices, the thrill of sudden laughter, and the delicious accompaniment of soft, sensuous music completed the charm of the room. To eat in such surroundings was as far beyond the famous flower-crowned feasts of Rome and Greece as the east is from the west. It was impossible to resist its influence. From the point of the senses, the soul was drinking life out of a cup of overflowing delight. And it was only natural that in their hearts both Tyrrel and Ethel should make a swift, though silent, comparison between this feast of sensation and flow of human attraction and the still, sweet order of the Rawdon dining-room, with its noiseless service, and its latticed windows open to all the wandering scents and songs of the garden.

Perhaps the latter would have the sweetest and dearest and most abiding place in their hearts; but just in the present they were enthralled and excited by the beauty and good comradeship of the social New York dinner function. Their eyes were shining, their hearts thrilling, they went to their own apartments hand in hand, buoyant, vivacious, feeling that life was good and love unchangeable. And the windows being open, they walked to one and stood looking out upon the avenue. All signs of commerce had gone from the beautiful street, but it was busy and noisy with the traffic of pleasure, and the hum of multitudes, the rattle of carriages,

Amelia E. Barr

the rush of autos, the light, hurrying footsteps of pleasure-seekers insistently demanded their sympathy.

"We cannot go out to-night," said Ethel. "We are both more weary than we know."

"No, we cannot go to-night; but, oh, Ethel, we are in New York again! Is not that joy enough? I am so happy! I am so happy. We are in New York again! There is no city like it in all the world. Men live here, they work here, they enjoy here. How happy, how busy we are going to be, Ethel!"

During these joyful, hopeful expectations he was walking up and down the room, his eyes dilating with rapture, and Ethel closed the window and joined him. They magnified their joy, they wondered at it, they were sure no one before them had ever loved as they loved. "And we are going to live here, Ethel; going to have our home here! Upon my honor, I cannot speak the joy I feel, but"—and he went impetuously to the piano and opened it—"but I can perhaps sing it—

"'There is not a spot in this wide-peopled earth
So dear to the heart as the Land of our Birth;
'Tis the home of our childhood, the beautiful spot
Which Memory retains when all else is forgot.
May the blessing of God ever hallow the sod,
And its valleys and hills by our children be trod!

"'May Columbia long lift her white crest o'er the wave,
The birthplace of science and the home of the brave.
In her cities may peace and prosperity dwell,
And her daughters in virtue and beauty excel.
May the blessing of God ever hallow the sod,
And its valleys and hills by our children be trod.'"

With the patriotic music warbling in his throat he turned to

Ethel, and looked at her as a lover can, and she answered the look; and thus leaning toward each other in visible beauty and affection their new life began. Between smiles and kisses they sat speaking, not of the past with all its love and loveliness, but of the high things calling to them from the future, the work and duties of life set to great ends both for public and private good. And as they thus communed Tyrrel took his wife's hand and slowly turned on her finger the plain gold wedding ring behind its barrier of guarding gems.

"Ethel," he said tenderly, "what enchantments are in this ring of gold! What romances I used to weave around it, and, dearest, it has turned every Romance into Reality."

"And, Tyrrel, it will also turn all our Realities into Romances. Nothing in our life will ever become common. Love will glorify everything."

"And we shall always love as we love now?"

"We shall love far better, far stronger, far more tenderly."

"Even to the end of our lives, Ethel?"

"Yes, to the very end."

Amelia E. Barr

CHAPTER XIII

A PAUSE of blissful silence followed this assurance. It was broken by a little exclamation from Ethel. "Oh, dear," she said, "how selfishly thoughtless my happiness makes me! I have forgotten to tell you, until this moment, that I have a letter from Dora. It was sent to grandmother's care, and I got it this afternoon; also one from Lucy Rawdon. The two together bring Dora's affairs, I should say, to a pleasanter termination than we could have hoped for."

"Where is the Enchantress?"

"In Paris at present."

"I expected that answer."

"But listen, she is living the quietest of lives; the most devoted daughter cannot excel her."

"Is she her own authority for that astonishing statement? Do you believe it?"

"Yes, under the circumstances. Mr. Denning went to Paris for a critical and painful operation, and Dora is giving all her love and time toward making his convalescence as pleasant as it can be. In fact, her description of their life in the pretty chateau they have rented outside of Paris is quite idyllic. When her father is able to travel they are going to Algiers for the winter, and will return to New York about next May. Dora says she never intends to leave America again."

"Where is her husband? Keeping watch on the French chateau?"

"That is over. Mr. Denning persuaded Dora to write a statement of all the facts concerning the birth of the child. She told her husband the name under which they traveled, the names of the ship, the captain, and the ship's doctor, and Mrs. Denning authenticated the statement; but, oh, what a mean, suspicious creature Mostyn is!"

"What makes you reiterate that description of him?"

"He was quite unable to see any good or kind intent in this paper. He proved its correctness, and then wrote Mr. Denning a very contemptible letter."

"Which was characteristic enough. What did he say?"

"That the amende honorable was too late; that he supposed Dora wished to have the divorce proceedings stopped and be reinstated as his wife, but he desired the whole Denning family to understand that was now impossible; he was 'fervently, feverishly awaiting his freedom, which he expected at any hour.' He said it was 'sickening to remember the weariness of body and soul Dora had given him about a non-existing child, and though this could never be atoned for, he did think he ought to be refunded the money Dora's contemptible revenge had cost him.'"

"How could he? How could he?"

"Of course Mr. Denning sent him a check, a pretty large one, I dare say. And I suppose he has his freedom by this time, unless he has married again."

"He will never marry again."

"Indeed, that is the strange part of the story. It was because he wanted to marry again that he was 'fervently, feverishly awaiting his freedom.'"

"I can hardly believe it, Ethel. What does Dora say?"

"I have the news from Lucy. She says when Mostyn was ignored by everyone in the neighborhood, one woman stood up for him almost passionately. Do you remember Miss Sadler?"

"That remarkable governess of the Surreys? Why, Ethel, she is the very ugliest woman I ever saw."

"She is so ugly that she is fascinating. If you see her one minute you can never forget her, and she is brains to her finger tips. She ruled everyone at Surrey House. She was Lord Surrey's secretary and Lady Surrey's adviser. She educated the children, and they adored her; she ruled the servants, and they obeyed her with fear and trembling. Nothing was done in Surrey House without her approval. And if her face was not handsome, she had a noble presence and a manner that was irresistible."

"And she took Mostyn's part?"

"With enthusiasm. She abused Dora individually, and American women generally. She pitied Mr. Mostyn, and made others do so; and when she perceived there would be but a shabby and tardy restoration for him socially, she advised him to shake off the dust of his feet from Monk-

Rawdon, and begin life in some more civilized place. And in order that he might do so, she induced Lord Surrey to get him a very excellent civil appointment in Calcutta."

"Then he is going to India?"

"He is probably now on the way there. He sold the Mostyn estate—"

"I can hardly believe it."

"He sold it to John Thomas Rawdon. John Thomas told me it belonged to Rawdon until the middle of the seventeenth century, and he meant to have it back. He has got it."

"Miss Sadler must be a witch."

"She is a sensible, practical woman, who knows how to manage men. She has soothed Mostyn's wounded pride with appreciative flattery and stimulated his ambition. She has promised him great things in India, and she will see that he gets them."

"He must be completely under her control."

"She will never let him call his soul his own, but she will manage his affairs to perfection. And Dora is forever rid of that wretched influence. The man can never again come between her and her love; never again come between her and happiness. There will be the circumference of the world as a barrier."

"There will be Jane Sadler as a barrier. She will be sufficient. The Woman Between will annihilate The Man Between. Dora is now safe. What will she do with herself?"

"She will come back to New York and be a social power.

She is young, beautiful, rich, and her father has tremendous financial influence. Social affairs are ruled by finance. I should not wonder to see her in St. Jude's, a devotee and eminent for good works."

"And if Basil Stanhope should return?"

"Poor Basil—he is dead."

"How do you know that?"

"What DO you mean, Tyrrel?"

"Are you sure Basil is dead? What proof have you?"

"You must be dreaming! Of course he is dead! His friend came and told me so—told me everything."

"Is that all?"

"There were notices in the papers."

"Is that all?"

"Mr. Denning must have known it when he stopped divorce proceedings."

"Doubtless he believed it; he wished to do so."

"Tyrrel, tell me what you mean."

"I always wondered about his death rather than believed in it. Basil had a consuming sense of honor and affection for the Church and its sacred offices. He would have died willingly rather than drag them into the mire of a divorce court. When the fear became certainty he disappeared—really died to all his previous life."

"But I cannot conceive of Basil lying for any purpose."

"He disappeared. His family and friends took on themselves the means they thought most likely to make that disappearance a finality."

"Have you heard anything, seen anything?"

"One night just before I left the West a traveler asked me for a night's lodging. He had been prospecting in British America in the region of the Klondike, and was full of incidental conversation. Among many other things he told me of a wonderful sermon he had heard from a young man in a large mining camp. I did not give the story any attention at the time, but after he had gone away it came to me like a flash of light that the preacher was Basil Stanhope."

"Oh, Tyrrel, if it was—if it was! What a beautiful dream! But it is only a dream. If it could be true, would he forgive Dora? Would he come back to her?"

"No!" Tyrrel's voice was positive and even stern. "No, he could never come back to her. She might go to him. She left him without any reason. I do not think he would care to see her again."

"I would say no more, Tyrrel. I do not think as you do. It is a dream, a fancy, just an imagination. But if it were true, Basil would wish no pilgrimage of abasement. He would say to her, 'Dear one, HUSH! Love is here, travel-stained, sore and weary, but so happy to welcome you!' And he would open all his great, sweet heart to her. May I tell Dora some day what you have thought and said? It will be something good for her to dream about."

"Do you think she cares? Did she ever love him?"

"He was her first love. She loved him once with all her heart. If it would be right—safe, I mean, to tell Dora—"

"On this subject there is so much NOT to say. I would never speak of it."

"It may be a truth"

"Then it is among those truths that should be held back, and it is likely only a trick of my imagination, a supposition, a fancy."

A miracle! And of two miracles I prefer the least, and that is that Basil is dead. Your young preacher is a dream; and, oh, Tyrrel, I am so tired! It has been such a long, long, happy day! I want to sleep. My eyes are shutting as I talk to you. Such a long, long, happy day!"

"And so many long, happy days to come, dearest."

"So many," she answered, as she took Tyrrel's hand, and lifted her fur and fan and gloves. "What were those lines we read together the night before we were married? I forget, I am so tired. I know that life should have many a hope and aim, duties enough, and little cares, and now be quiet, and now astir, till God's hand beckoned us unawares—"

The rest was inaudible. But between that long, happy day and the present time there has been an arc of life large enough to place the union of Tyrrel and Ethel Rawdon among those blessed bridals that are

"The best of life's romances."

Other books by this author

The Bow of Orange Ribbon

The Maid of Maiden Lane

The Squire of Sandal-Side

A Knight of the Nets

Amelia E. Barr

Choose from Thousands of 1stWorldLibrary Classics By

A. M. Barnard
Ada Leverson
Adolphus William Ward
Aesop
Agatha Christie
Alexander Aaronsohn
Alexander Kielland
Alexandre Dumas
Alfred Gatty
Alfred Ollivant
Alice Duer Miller
Alice Turner Curtis
Alice Dunbar
Allen Chapman
Alleyne Ireland
Ambrose Bierce
Amelia E. Barr
Amory H. Bradford
Andrew Lang
Andrew McFarland Davis
Andy Adams
Angela Brazil
Anna Alice Chapin
Anna Sewell
Annie Besant
Annie Hamilton Donnell
Annie Payson Call
Annie Roe Carr
Annonaymous
Anton Chekhov
Archibald Lee Fletcher
Arnold Bennett
Arthur C. Benson
Arthur Conan Doyle
Arthur M. Winfield
Arthur Ransome
Arthur Schnitzler
Arthur Train
Atticus
B. H. Baden-Powell
B. M. Bower
B. C. Chatterjee
Baroness Emmuska Orczy
Baroness Orczy
Basil King
Bayard Taylor
Ben Macomber
Bertha Muzzy Bower
Bjornstjerne Bjornson

Booth Tarkington
Boyd Cable
Bram Stoker
C. Collodi
C. E. Orr
C. M. Ingleby
Carolyn Wells
Catherine Parr Traill
Charles A. Eastman
Charles Amory Beach
Charles Dickens
Charles Dudley Warner
Charles Farrar Browne
Charles Ives
Charles Kingsley
Charles Klein
Charles Hanson Towne
Charles Lathrop Pack
Charles Romyn Dake
Charles Whibley
Charles Willing Beale
Charlotte M. Braeme
Charlotte M. Yonge
Charlotte Perkins Stetson
Clair W. Hayes
Clarence Day Jr.
Clarence E. Mulford
Clemence Housman
Confucius
Coningsby Dawson
Cornelis DeWitt Wilcox
Cyril Burleigh
D. H. Lawrence
Daniel Defoe
David Garnett
Dinah Craik
Don Carlos Janes
Donald Keyhoe
Dorothy Kilner
Dougan Clark
Douglas Fairbanks
E. Nesbit
E. P. Roe
E. Phillips Oppenheim
E. S. Brooks
Earl Barnes
Edgar Rice Burroughs
Edith Van Dyne
Edith Wharton

Edward Everett Hale
Edward J. O'Biren
Edward S. Ellis
Edwin L. Arnold
Eleanor Atkins
Eleanor Hallowell Abbott
Eliot Gregory
Elizabeth Gaskell
Elizabeth McCracken
Elizabeth Von Arnim
Ellem Key
Emerson Hough
Emilie F. Carlen
Emily Bronte
Emily Dickinson
Enid Bagnold
Enilor Macartney Lane
Erasmus W. Jones
Ernie Howard Pie
Ethel May Dell
Ethel Turner
Ethel Watts Mumford
Eugene Sue
Eugenie Foa
Eugene Wood
Eustace Hale Ball
Evelyn Everett-green
Everard Cotes
F. H. Cheley
F. J. Cross
F. Marion Crawford
Fannie E. Newberry
Federick Austin Ogg
Ferdinand Ossendowski
Fergus Hume
Florence A. Kilpatrick
Fremont B. Deering
Francis Bacon
Francis Darwin
Frances Hodgson Burnett
Frances Parkinson Keyes
Frank Gee Patchin
Frank Harris
Frank Jewett Mather
Frank L. Packard
Frank V. Webster
Frederic Stewart Isham
Frederick Trevor Hill
Frederick Winslow Taylor

Friedrich Kerst
Friedrich Nietzsche
Fyodor Dostoyevsky
G. A. Henty
G. K. Chesterton
Gabrielle E. Jackson
Garrett P. Serviss
Gaston Leroux
George A. Warren
George Ade
Geroge Bernard Shaw
George Cary Eggleston
George Durston
George Ebers
George Eliot
George Gissing
George MacDonald
George Meredith
George Orwell
George Sylvester Viereck
George Tucker
George W. Cable
George Wharton James
Gertrude Atherton
Gordon Casserly
Grace E. King
Grace Gallatin
Grace Greenwood
Grant Allen
Guillermo A. Sherwell
Gulielma Zollinger
Gustav Flaubert
H. A. Cody
H. B. Irving
H. C. Bailey
H. G. Wells
H. H. Munro
H. Irving Hancock
H. R. Naylor
H. Rider Haggard
H. W. C. Davis
Haldeman Julius
Hall Caine
Hamilton Wright Mabie
Hans Christian Andersen
Harold Avery
Harold McGrath
Harriet Beecher Stowe
Harry Castlemon
Harry Coghill
Harry Houidini

Hayden Carruth
Helent Hunt Jackson
Helen Nicolay
Hendrik Conscience
Hendy David Thoreau
Henri Barbusse
Henrik Ibsen
Henry Adams
Henry Ford
Henry Frost
Henry James
Henry Jones Ford
Henry Seton Merriman
Henry W Longfellow
Herbert A. Giles
Herbert Carter
Herbert N. Casson
Herman Hesse
Hildegard G. Frey
Homer
Honore De Balzac
Horace B. Day
Horace Walpole
Horatio Alger Jr.
Howard Pyle
Howard R. Garis
Hugh Lofting
Hugh Walpole
Humphry Ward
Ian Maclaren
Inez Haynes Gillmore
Irving Bacheller
Isabel Cecilia Williams
Isabel Hornibrook
Israel Abrahams
Ivan Turgenev
J. G.Austin
J. Henri Fabre
J. M. Barrie
J. M. Walsh
J. Macdonald Oxley
J. R. Miller
J. S. Fletcher
J. S. Knowles
J. Storer Clouston
J. W. Duffield
Jack London
Jacob Abbott
James Allen
James Andrews
James Baldwin

James Branch Cabell
James DeMille
James Joyce
James Lane Allen
James Lane Allen
James Oliver Curwood
James Oppenheim
James Otis
James R. Driscoll
Jane Abbott
Jane Austen
Jane L. Stewart
Janet Aldridge
Jens Peter Jacobsen
Jerome K. Jerome
Jessie Graham Flower
John Buchan
John Burroughs
John Cournos
John F. Kennedy
John Gay
John Glasworthy
John Habberton
John Joy Bell
John Kendrick Bangs
John Milton
John Philip Sousa
John Taintor Foote
Jonas Lauritz Idemil Lie
Jonathan Swift
Joseph A. Altsheler
Joseph Carey
Joseph Conrad
Joseph E. Badger Jr
Joseph Hergesheimer
Joseph Jacobs
Jules Vernes
Julian Hawthrone
Julie A Lippmann
Justin Huntly McCarthy
Kakuzo Okakura
Karle Wilson Baker
Kate Chopin
Kenneth Grahame
Kenneth McGaffey
Kate Langley Bosher
Kate Langley Bosher
Katherine Cecil Thurston
Katherine Stokes
L. A. Abbot
L. T. Meade

L. Frank Baum
Latta Griswold
Laura Dent Crane
Laura Lee Hope
Laurence Housman
Lawrence Beasley
Leo Tolstoy
Leonid Andreyev
Lewis Carroll
Lewis Sperry Chafer
Lilian Bell
Lloyd Osbourne
Louis Hughes
Louis Joseph Vance
Louis Tracy
Louisa May Alcott
Lucy Fitch Perkins
Lucy Maud Montgomery
Luther Benson
Lydia Miller Middleton
Lyndon Orr
M. Corvus
M. H. Adams
Margaret E. Sangster
Margret Howth
Margaret Vandercook
Margaret W. Hungerford
Margret Penrose
Maria Edgeworth
Maria Thompson Daviess
Mariano Azuela
Marion Polk Angellotti
Mark Overton
Mark Twain
Mary Austin
Mary Catherine Crowley
Mary Cole
Mary Hastings Bradley
Mary Roberts Rinehart
Mary Rowlandson
M. Wollstonecraft Shelley
Maud Lindsay
Max Beerbohm
Myra Kelly
Nathaniel Hawthrone
Nicolo Machiavelli
O. F. Walton
Oscar Wilde

Owen Johnson
P. G. Wodehouse
Paul and Mabel Thorne
Paul G. Tomlinson
Paul Severing
Percy Brebner
Percy Keese Fitzhugh
Peter B. Kyne
Plato
Quincy Allen
R. Derby Holmes
R. L. Stevenson
R. S. Ball
Rabindranath Tagore
Rahul Alvares
Ralph Bonehill
Ralph Henry Barbour
Ralph Victor
Ralph Waldo Emmerson
Rene Descartes
Ray Cummings
Rex Beach
Rex E. Beach
Richard Harding Davis
Richard Jefferies
Richard Le Gallienne
Robert Barr
Robert Frost
Robert Gordon Anderson
Robert L. Drake
Robert Lansing
Robert Lynd
Robert Michael Ballantyne
Robert W. Chambers
Rosa Nouchette Carey
Rudyard Kipling
Saint Augustine
Samuel B. Allison
Samuel Hopkins Adams
Sarah Bernhardt
Sarah C. Hallowell
Selma Lagerlof
Sherwood Anderson
Sigmund Freud
Standish O'Grady
Stanley Weyman
Stella Benson
Stella M. Francis

Stephen Crane
Stewart Edward White
Stijn Streuvels
Swami Abhedananda
Swami Parmananda
T. S. Ackland
T. S. Arthur
The Princess Der Ling
Thomas A. Janvier
Thomas A Kempis
Thomas Anderton
Thomas Bailey Aldrich
Thomas Bulfinch
Thomas De Quincey
Thomas Dixon
Thomas H. Huxley
Thomas Hardy
Thomas More
Thornton W. Burgess
U. S. Grant
Upton Sinclair
Valentine Williams
Various Authors
Vaughan Kester
Victor Appleton
Victor G. Durham
Victoria Cross
Virginia Woolf
Wadsworth Camp
Walter Camp
Walter Scott
Washington Irving
Wilbur Lawton
Wilkie Collins
Willa Cather
Willard F. Baker
William Dean Howells
William le Queux
W. Makepeace Thackeray
William W. Walter
William Shakespeare
Winston Churchill
Yei Theodora Ozaki
Yogi Ramacharaka
Young E. Allison
Zane Grey